SOUL OF THE WITCH

WITCHES OF KEATING HOLLOW, BOOK 1

DEANNA CHASE

ABOUT THIS BOOK

Welcome to Keating Hollow, the village full of love, magic, and cupcakes, and where nothing is more important than family.

At age eighteen, after a potion tragically backfired, Abby Townsend left Keating Hollow and her magic behind to find redemption. Ten years later, after being summoned by her family, she's back. As soon as she drives into town, she's already plotting her inevitable exit, but she can't quite escape the pull of the tightly knit magical community or the soulful gaze of the one man she's never forgotten. And when an eight-year old witch not only leads her back to her magic, but also steals her heart, Abby's about to learn what it means to embrace the soul of a witch.

CHAPTER 1

*T*his *Way Lies Hallowed Ground.*

The familiar weathered sign meant Abby was only twenty miles from Keating Hollow, the hidden Northern California town that had been settled by witches almost a century ago. She turned off the highway onto the nondescript two-lane road and sat up, the weariness suddenly vanishing from her travel-worn body. She'd been driving for three days, dreading every moment of crossing into the quaint witch village. But now that she was here, a tingle of magic settled in her bones, and for just a split-second, peace washed over her.

She was home.

The peace vanished, replaced by the familiar anxiety that had sent her running across the country ten years ago. She tightened her fingers over the steering wheel as she remembered her one and only short visit at Christmas six years earlier. The trip had only been three days. Two days too long, if you asked Abby. It had just been too hard. Too many painful memories. Too much guilt. Too much everything.

"Relax," she said softly as she focused on the giant

redwoods, determined to block out the past. She couldn't change anything that happened back then or anything that had happened since. And she couldn't keep running forever. Not this time. Her sister had called and told her it was time to come home—Dad was sick. Tears stung the backs of her eyes, and she blinked them back.

Crying was not an option. Not now. And especially not in front of her dad. Later in the evening, after she'd sat at the kitchen table with her dad, lingering over a large mug of Grandma Harper's famous hot cocoa, then she could lock herself in the bathroom and fall apart in the shower.

The winding road straightened out, and the dense redwoods disappeared from her rearview mirror. She drove into the quaint little downtown area and on impulse, swung into a parking spot right in front of A Spoon Full of Magic. Taking a moment to stretch her aching legs, Abby watched the magical mixing cups weigh out ingredients and transfer them to copper bowls right in the front window. Her lips twitched into a small smile. Nobody made chocolate cheesecake tortes like Miss Maple.

Abby swept into the shop and breathed in the delicious sweet scents of caramel and chocolate. Her stomach growled as her mouth watered in anticipation.

"Abigail Townsend?" a high pitched voice called from behind the counter.

Abby glanced up and spotted a curvy redhead wrapped in a blue and white striped apron. Her hair was piled on the top of her head, and she wore stylish blue cat-eye glasses.

"Hi, Shannon," Abby said, biting back a scowl as she gazed at her junior high nemesis. She'd always secretly hoped the girl who'd made her life miserable for six months would wind up with acne and frizzy hair. Unfortunately, the woman in front

SOUL OF THE WITCH

of her had flawless skin and silky smooth curls that were worthy of a shampoo commercial.

"Gosh. I haven't seen you since..." Shannon's tanned face turned to ash as she swallowed her next words.

"Not since Charlotte's memorial," Abby said, her tone void of any emotion.

"Right. Of course." Shannon averted her eyes as she wiped her hands on a towel. When she glanced back up, she had a pasted on smile. "It's good to see you in town. Did you just get in? Yvette mentioned you were coming for a visit."

"Yes, just rolled in this minute and decided I couldn't go another day without Miss Maple's chocolate caramel bars."

"Excellent." Shannon whipped out a glitter-covered turquoise wand and pointed it at the display case. A second later, a half-dozen bars floated out and stacked themselves into a small white box.

"Oh, that's too many," Abigail protested. "I was only going to get one."

"These are on the house. Welcome home present." A spool of turquoise ribbon right behind Shannon spun rapidly and then stopped, leaving a hank of about two feet. Shannon turned, snipped the piece off, and quickly wrapped it around the box, tying it off deftly with a perfectly balanced bow. "Here you go," she said, pushing it toward Abby.

"You really don't have to do that," Abby said, shaking her head.

Shannon waved an unconcerned hand. "Take them home to Lin. I know they're his favorite."

Abby started to deny the offer but quickly changed course and nodded instead. The bars *were* Lincoln Townsend's favorite, and if Shannon wanted to do something nice for her father, Abby certainly wasn't going to refuse. "Thank you. That's very kind."

"Lin does so much for everyone. It's the least I can do. Now, anything else I can get for you?"

Abigail ordered a full-size chocolate cheesecake torte and a tin of Miss Maple's special cocoa mix. After she paid, she grabbed the torte box and reached for the small bag of chocolate treats and cocoa.

"Wait." Shannon reached below the counter and produced a couple packages of cinnamon sticks. "Take these, too." With a small sympathetic smile, she added, "Good for healing."

The sob Abby had been holding back the last three days clogged her throat again. "Thank you," she forced out, her voice raspy and too full of emotion.

"It's going to be okay," Shannon said, placing her hand over Abby's. "I can feel it."

Abby stared at the genuine sincerity in the other woman's eyes and felt some small piece of her heart mend. She'd almost forgotten that in Keating Hollow, kindness bred its own very real magic. "I hope so." She turned to go, but as she pulled the door open, she glanced back and smiled. "Thanks, Shannon. I needed to hear that."

"You're very welcome. Enjoy your homecoming."

Abby nodded and stepped back out onto Main Street, the bell on the door clanging behind her. She paused and sucked in a deep breath, letting the faint redwood-scented air wash over her before climbing back into her car.

She'd just jammed the key into the ignition when someone blaring "Fireball" by Pitbull pulled into the space beside her, honking incessantly.

Beep, beep, beeeeep.

Abby glanced over, ready to tell the motorist to keep their pants on, but then froze in surprise as she took in the six-seater golf cart, its flashing strobe lights, and the crazy woman frantically waving at her.

Abby pushed her door open and gasped, "Wanda?"

"Abby!" The curvy woman flipped a switch on the dash, causing the music to vanish. Then she hopped out of her party cart and ran over to Abby, engulfing her in an all-encompassing hug. "Oh my goddess, I can't believe you're finally here. I've been waiting all day for this."

Warmth spread through Abby as she hugged her old high school friend tightly. "What were you doing? Staking out the city limits until I rolled into town?"

"Ha! Don't flatter yourself." Wanda pulled back and grinned. "I was tooling down to the liquor store to restock the wine fridge when I saw you sneaking out of Miss Maple's." She glanced through the window of Abby's Mazda CX-3. "Chocolate cheesecake torte. You never could resist that yummy goodness, could you?"

Abby laughed. "Not when it comes to Miss Maple's cheesecake." Peering over Wanda's shoulder, Abby raised a curious eyebrow. "That's some ride you've got there."

"Isn't it?" Wanda walked back around the cart and slid back into the driver's seat. "Check this out." She turned the key then pushed a button on the dash. The lights flashed purple just as Prince blared over the surround sound speakers. Pumping her eyebrows, she added, "Sweet right?"

"Freakin' awesome is more like it," Abby said, half tempted to jump into the cart with her. If she hadn't needed to get home to see her dad, she would have.

A wicked gleam lit Wanda's hazel gaze. "A few of us girls are racing tonight at midnight. Want to join us?"

"Golf cart races?" Abby laughed.

"Hell, yes. Add in a little mermaid water and it's the most fun you can have with your clothes on. Trust me. You'll love it."

Chuckling, Abby shook her head. "I'd love to. But it's my first night back and..."

"I understand. Just wanted to extend the invitation. Next time, huh?"

"You bet," Abby said. "And I'm holding you to that mermaid water."

Wanda winked. "Give me a call after you're settled in, and we'll get the girls together for another race. In the meantime, I'm always up for taking this baby out for a spin down by the lake. All right?"

"Sounds great, Wanda!" Abby called after her as Wanda backed out into the street.

Wanda bounced up and down in the seat to the music, enjoying life to its fullest as she motored down the road.

Feeling an odd sense of loss, Abby climbed back into her SUV, buckled in, and carefully pulled back out onto Main Street.

Abby passed her favorite used bookstore a few shops down on the right, the window displays already decorated with fall gourds and wheat stalks. She smiled when she spotted Woodlines and Cozy Cave, the two rival restaurants in town. They were directly across the street from one another and both had signs that read *Voted Best Crab Cakes in Town*.

A tiny thread of peace wound around her heart. It was good to know nothing ever changed in Keating Hollow.

Well, almost nothing.

The familiar yellow and green sign of her father's brewery came into view: *Townsend's Keating Hollow Brewery*. But instead of her father's vintage, nineteen fifty-eight red GMC truck sitting out front, there was a midnight blue Jeep Wrangler parked in its spot.

"Who does that belong to?" she muttered. Then her eyes widened as a tall, dark-haired man with a lopsided smile she'd know anywhere walked out of the store and over to an idling delivery truck. He was carrying a clipboard and wearing a black polo shirt, the same one she'd seen her father wear thousands of times before.

Her heart fluttered and butterflies took over her stomach.

Clay Garrison, her first kiss, first love, first everything, was back here in Keating Hollow, working at her father's brewery.

Holy cow bells. She glanced in her rearview mirror, checking out her mussed blond hair, haphazardly tied into a bun, and her fatigued, road-weary face. The light trace of makeup she'd slapped on over twelve hours ago was long gone. She had to get out of there before Clay spotted her looking like she'd spent the night sleeping under a bridge.

She stepped on the gas and promptly came to a screeching, abrupt halt, the seatbelt the only thing keeping her from flying into the windshield, as the sound of metal on metal rang in her ears.

CHAPTER 2

"*O*uch!" she cried, pressing her hand to her chest where the seatbelt dug into her flesh. "Son of a... Oh no!" She stared at the crumpled white Mini Cooper in front of her. With her blood racing and her pulse pounding in her ears, she hastily undid the seatbelt and flew out of the car, just as a shaken teenager stumbled from the Mini Cooper.

"Oh my goddess," Abby said, her hands trembling with shock from the accident. "Are you okay? I'm so sorry."

The tiny brunette nodded, her dark curls blowing in the early evening breeze. "I think so." The teenager turned and looked at the back end of her car. Her dazed expression turned to shocked horror as she slapped her hand over her open mouth. In a muffled whisper she said, "My aunt is going to kill me."

"Don't worry," Abby said quickly, trying to reassure the girl. "This was all my fault, and I have insurance. A little time in the body shop and everything will be as good as new."

But the teenager shook her head. "No. You don't

understand." Tears formed in her Kewpie doll eyes. "I wasn't supposed to be driving her car."

"Oh, hell," Abigail said with a sigh.

"Is everyone all right? I've already called the sheriff's office," a deep voice that made Abby's skin tingle asked from behind her. She glanced over at him, praying the asphalt would open up and let the earth swallow her whole. Good gracious he was gorgeous. Gone was the tall, lanky teenager she'd loved so fiercely, replaced by a man who'd grown into his frame with a broad chest and well-defined shoulders.

The teenager shook her head again and Clay strode over, placing his hands on her shoulders. "Where are you hurt?"

The teenager pointed toward me. "She killed the Mini."

"What?" He glanced back at me briefly then turned to her again. "But you're not hurt?"

"Not physically. But—"

Clay cut the teen off as he turned back to Abby, concern shining in his beautiful brown eyes. "Abigail. Hello."

Abby almost sighed like the lovesick teenager she used to be. Instead, she waved her fingers at him. "Hi, Clay. It's been a while, huh?"

His expression instantly went blank. "Yeah. A while." He lowered his gaze and slowly scanned her body.

She glanced down at her frayed yoga pants and white T-shirt, noting the mustard stain just above her left breast. *Perfect*, she thought. Just the way every girl imagines being reunited with the one who got away. Talk about a cruel joke. Someone could make a movie about them and title it *Slobby and the Beautiful Beast*.

"How about you? Any broken bones, bumps, or bruises?" he asked.

"No, just my car." Abby grimaced as she turned back to the teenager, who was frantically texting away on her phone.

"We should move these to the side of the road while we wait."

The teenager's head snapped up. She glanced first at Abby, then at Clay, then at the line of traffic forming behind them. "Right."

Abby returned to her car, shoved the key into the ignition, and tried turning the engine over.

Click, click, click, click, click.

"Oh, come on," Abby said and tried again. Nothing.

Clay walked over to her door and leaned in through the open window. "Problem?"

"Sounds like I killed the battery. You don't suppose Miss Mini Cooper would help me jump it do you?"

They both glanced toward the other car just in time to see the Mini Cooper dart off down the road and disappear around a corner.

When Clay turned his attention back to Abby, she stared at him in disbelief and asked, "Did that just really happen? Did she just take off? I haven't even given her my insurance information yet."

"Maybe she circling and coming right back," he said with a shrug.

Abby glanced over her shoulder, looking for the little car, but all she saw was a traffic jam of frustrated drivers as they cautiously used the oncoming lane to ease around her. "Crap."

"Put the car in neutral," Clay said. "We need to push you out of the way."

She did as he requested then opened the door and got out. While Clay pushed from behind, she pushed from the driver's side, steering the small SUV into an empty parking spot. The cars behind her honked their appreciation as they sped by.

Clay, appearing as if he hadn't exerted one ounce of effort, joined her on the sidewalk. They both stared at her smashed hood. Even if the Mini Cooper hadn't taken off, there was no hope of getting a jumpstart. The hood wasn't opening without the help from a good body shop technician.

Abby closed her eyes for a moment then turned to Clay. "So, how long have you been back in town?"

"A couple years. You?" he asked without looking at her.

"About twenty minutes now."

He glanced her way, his lips twitching into a half smile. "That's some homecoming."

"You're telling me." Abby let out an exaggerated sigh. "I better call Yvette. Everyone's probably waiting for me." She pulled out her phone, but Clay's intense gaze seared straight through her, momentarily paralyzing her. The town ceased to exist, sounds of the traffic faded away, and all that was left was Clay. She careened forward, as if caught in his magnetism, and unconsciously licked her lips.

He cleared his throat. "I thought you were going to call Yvette."

"Right." Taking a step back, she pulled up her sister's number and hit Call. It went straight to voicemail. Abby sucked in a calming breath. "Vette?" she said into the phone. "There's been an accident. I'm fine, but I'm going to be a little late. Call me when you get this." She ended the call and shoved the phone back into her pocket.

"You drove all the way from Louisiana?" Clay asked, gesturing to her license plate. "That's a hell of a haul for a family visit isn't it?"

"I—"

"Mr. Garrison," a man in a brown police uniform called as he crossed the street. "There you are. What happened to the accident you called in?"

Clay waved at me. "Abby here rear-ended someone in a

Mini Cooper, but the girl took off without leaving any identifying information."

"Abigail Townsend," the police officer said, shaking his head in disapproval. Abby recognized him as one of Yvette's former classmates, Pauly Putzner. He was three years older than her, had asked her out once right before she and Clay had officially started dating, and had gained what Abby estimated at about fifty pounds. And if that wasn't enough, he was suffering from early-onset balding. "Looks like nothing's changed since you hightailed it out of here a decade ago. Still reckless I see."

Abby's entire body heated with both embarrassment and rage. She curled her fingers into fists and focused on *not* telling him where he could shove the night stick strapped to his duty belt.

"Abby's not the one that drove off, Pauly," Clay said, shaking his head and not bothering to hide the irritation in his tone. "Maybe you should take our statements before you go making judgments."

Pauly let out a grunt of disapproval, but pulled out a small notebook. A few minutes later, having apparently gotten all the details he deemed important, he asked for Abby's license and insurance card. After she handed both to him, he let out another snort of derision. "New Orleans? Figures. I hear that town is a beacon for the depraved."

"Hey!" Abby said, hands on her hips. "What's that supposed to mean?"

Clay wrapped an arm around her shoulders and pulled her in so she was pressed up against his lean, muscular body. *Aphrodite and Zeus*, she thought, *this man is pure heaven.*

"Officer Putzner," Clay said, his eyes narrowed. "Perhaps you could just stick to filing a report and lose the commentary."

"Right." Putzner chuckled as he looked from Clay to Abby.

"I forgot you two had a thing once." He turned his gaze to Abby. "Too bad that didn't work out. Clay here could've probably helped you work out some of those issues."

Abby envisioned hauling off and smacking the officer right in the kisser... even though she secretly admitted he was probably right.

Clay had always been her rock right up until the shit had hit the fan. Being in his arms and breathing in his scent of soap and a hint of fresh earth made her feel as if she'd never left all those years ago, like they'd never broken up and Clay had never married another woman.

Married. Right. Abigail shifted to the left and disengaged from Clay's protective embrace. Clearing her throat, she said, "Are we done here?"

"For now," Putzner said, eyeing her with suspicion. "Just keep your nose and your magic to yourself while you're in town, Miss Townsend. We don't want any more trouble around here."

Abby gritted her teeth, wishing she had the ability to curse his privates. How satisfying would it be if he woke up tomorrow with a shrunken penis? Her lips curved into a smile at the thought. But she only nodded and stayed silent as he sauntered off down the street.

"What were you thinking just then?" Clay asked.

"Nothing."

He chuckled. "With that wicked smile? Bull. You were definitely thinking something."

She blinked up at him then laughed. "Let's just say that if I had the power of transfiguration, he'd need a magnifying glass to find his equipment the next time he needs to relieve himself."

"That's the Abby I know and love," he said, still chuckling.

But when his eyes met hers, he immediately sobered and averted his gaze.

All the joy from being around him fled, and Abby pressed a hand to her abdomen, feeling as if she'd been sucker punched right in the gut. It wasn't nearly as bad as when she'd left him all those years ago, but it was an echo of the pain that had never left her. She turned her back on Clay, afraid her expression would give her away.

Pink's voice suddenly filled the silence as she sang about getting the party started, and Abby was relieved to see Wanda's party cart pulling in right next to her smashed SUV.

The music vanished, and Wanda said, "Hey, girl. Mindy Jo over at the wine bar told me someone from Louisiana had been in an accident. I knew it had to be you. You okay?"

"Fine," Abby said, grateful for the distraction. "Car's dead, though. I'm waiting for Yvette to call me back."

"She's been called into the fire station to help with a few brush fires near old man Hamilton's place. Need a ride somewhere?"

"Yes," Abby said without hesitation, pushing back the worry trying to creep into her thoughts. Her sister Yvette was a fire witch. Her ability to control the element had kept their county from burning during the dry fall months year after year. "Can you take me to my dad's?"

"Sure. Hop in."

"Great." Abby reached into the passenger side of the SUV and grabbed her purse and the sweets she'd purchase from A Spoon Full of Magic. And when she turned to head to Wanda's cart, Clay was right there behind her.

He peered into the back windows. "You sure don't travel light, do you?"

Abby chuckled. "No, not this time. I'm not sure how long I'm going to be here, and I still have a soap making business to run. I considered flying and shipping my supplies, but in the end I figured it would be easier to just drive." She gave him a wry smile. "Turns out maybe I shouldn't be driving at all."

"Maybe just not gawking at the scenery," he said with a teasing smile.

Oh hell. She closed her eyes. He'd caught her staring at him. Well, dammit, it wasn't her fault he looked even better than he did ten years ago. He should be required to wear a warning label or something.

"You should probably get going. I'm sure your dad is anxious to see you," he said, his voice suddenly low and full of sympathy as compassion shone in his dark eyes.

He knows, she thought, and had to glance away.

"I'm sure he is," she agreed as she moved toward Wanda's golf cart. Did the entire town know her dad was sick? It was a high probability. She'd have to get used to the concerned citizens of the town giving her that look. But right now, with Clay appearing to see straight into her soul, it was too much.

"It was really good to see you, Abs," he said.

She glanced over her shoulder, unable to read his now closed-off expression. "You, too, Clay. Thanks for your help."

"No problem. Be safe out there, okay?"

"I'll try." Then she flashed him a quick smile and hurried over to Wanda and away from the one man who, after all those years, still managed to make her heart beat just a little bit faster.

CHAPTER 3

$\mathcal{C}$lay stood on the sidewalk watching as Wanda and Abigail rode off in the crazy golf cart and disappeared into the late-afternoon sunshine. He'd thought he was hallucinating again when he'd glanced up from his clipboard to see Abby staring at him. How many times had he envisioned her returning to town in the last two years? More than he could count. It was strange living in Keating Hollow without her.

It was the reason he'd left ten years ago, and the only reason he'd been reluctant to return. But circumstances had changed, making it clear it was time for him to come home. He hadn't regretted his decision to leave Los Angeles and return to the witch community he'd been a part of since his childhood, but that didn't mean being here without her had been easy. And judging by the way his heart had nearly burst out of his chest when Abby's car plowed into the Mini Cooper, it was clear nothing had changed when it came to how he felt about her. Not now and probably not ever.

"Dammit," he muttered, running a hand through his hair.

He could not afford to go down that road again. He had bigger issues to deal with. Getting distracted by someone who would just up and leave again wasn't something he was willing to risk.

He moved off the curb, intending to head back to the brewery, but when he stepped on something hard and uneven, he stopped and glanced down. Light shone off a piece of silver metal nearly blinding him. Squinting, he bent down and inspected the object.

A set of keys.

He picked them up, eyed the emblem on the key fob, and glanced at Abigail's SUV. Both had the Mazda emblem. Running his thumb over the Unlock button, he pushed and heard a double click, indicating the keys were a match. After relocking the car, he pocketed the keys and pulled out his phone. But before he could dial a call came in, and his phone started playing "Forget You" by Ceelo Green.

Clay gritted his teeth and answered. "What is it, Val?"

"Well hello to you, too, honey," she said sweetly. Loud voices chattered in the background over the bubble gum pop music she liked so much.

"Stop playing games. What did you need?" His fingers tightened around his phone so hard, he was amazed the plastic case hadn't cracked. "Is it Olive? Is she okay?"

"Stop being such an old man," she snapped, all the sweetness replaced by venom. "Olive is fine. I just called to say we're in Palm Springs on a shoot. Olive's staying with me for another week."

"We agreed to a two-week visit, Val. Not three," he said, careful to keep his tone steady. He'd learned from past experiences that blowing up at her only made her more likely to dig her heels in and do whatever she damn well pleased. "Olive needs to come home. She has school. You can't just disrupt her schedule like that."

18

"Why not? You did when you dragged her off to that godforsaken town in the middle of nowhere."

"You moved to Paris," he said through clenched teeth.

"Without us."

"I was only gone for six months. Jayzus, Clay. It's not like I ran off with another man."

Right. Clay chose to avoid that particular argument. He'd heard the rumors. Had lived the lonely nights when she'd been off 'modeling' for shoots that never seemed to result in a paycheck. "None of that matters now," he said, calmly. "Just bring Olive home, or tell me where you two are staying and I'll come get her."

"No. *She* has a job. One she wants to do. You're not taking this away from her. Not like you tried to do to me. I'll bring her home when it's done."

"*She* has a job? She, as in *Olive* has a job?" Clay barked into the phone.

Val didn't answer, and the chatter in the background had vanished. Clay pulled the phone away from his ear and scowled at the screen. Son of a witch. His ex had hung up on him. He called her back, but her phone went straight to voicemail. "Dammit!"

"Something wrong in Garrisonville?" a woman asked from behind him.

He glanced over his shoulder and spotted Yvette, Abigail's sister, standing on the sidewalk and holding a large bottle of water. Her jeans had black soot stains, but her Keating Hollow volunteer firefighter T-shirt was clean, as was the baseball cap covering her chestnut hair. "Isn't there always?"

She gave him a sympathetic smile. "Val being an uber-bitch again?"

"When isn't she?" He rolled his shoulders, trying to release the tension. "She just called to inform me she's keeping Olive

for another week so that Olive can finish some sort of shoot. I
don't know if it's a photography shoot, a commercial, or
something else. Apparently, Val seems to think she doesn't
need to consult me when it comes to our daughter."

"Ouch." Yvette frowned, placing her hands on her trim
waist. "I thought you decided to keep her out of the business?"

"I did. Val didn't."

"I hate to say it, Clay, but I really think you should consider
that lawyer. Until you get this custody thing worked out, she's
going to keep doing this to you."

"You're probably right," Clay said out of habit more than
anything else. Everyone in town had told him the same thing
more than once. The only problem was Val had connections he
didn't have. Her friends in the business had access to custody
lawyers who were real sharks. Expensive lawyers who'd wage a
battle he couldn't afford to fight. He'd been hoping he and Val
could work something out through mediation. Keep it simple,
do whatever was right for Olive. Two years ago, that had been
a fine solution. Val hadn't been interested in being a mother
anyway. But now? Clay was afraid Val only saw dollar signs
when she looked at their beautiful little girl.

When she'd called wanting time with Olive six months ago,
Clay had been relieved, though a little suspicious, and agreed
to shared custody. Olive would go see her on school breaks as
often as Val wanted her. His daughter needed her mother, and
he'd do whatever it took to make sure Olive got to spend time
with her.

Their first visit had been fairly normal. Val had taken Olive
to an audition, but Clay had assumed it was Val's audition
since she knew Clay wasn't crazy about his daughter being
anywhere near the entertainment industry, especially since she
was only eight years old. Now he wasn't so sure. Had Val been
grooming her these last months? Surely whatever shoot she'd

SOUL OF THE WITCH

booked for Olive hadn't been a fluke. Jobs didn't come that easily in Hollywood. An ache formed in the pit of his stomach, and he was afraid his worst suspicions were confirmed. He needed to talk to Olive, find out if this was something she wanted or if Val had forced it on her.

Yvette patted his arm. "Give Lorna a call. She knows how to handle these things."

Lorna was the town attorney. And while Clay respected the sweet older woman, he also knew that the high powered LA attorneys Val threatened to hire would eat her alive. "I'll consider it."

"Let us know if there is anything we can do." Yvette eyed the wrecked car. "What happened here?"

He raised an eyebrow. "You haven't checked your voicemail yet, have you?"

"No. I was putting out a fire." She patted her back pocket and produced a smart phone. As she checked her messages she asked Clay, "Want to give me the rundown?"

"Your sister rear-ended someone while checking me out." Clay couldn't help the pleased smile that tugged at his lips.

"Abigail? She made it to town?" Yvette's eyes widened. "Is everyone all right?"

"Yes, but that SUV is going to need some major work. After the accident, it refused to start. Wanda gave her a lift on her pimped-out golf cart."

Yvette snickered. "Of course she did. Well, that's one way to make an entrance back to the family farm." She was quiet for a moment, listening to her messages. Then she hit a button and pressed the phone to her ear once more. "Abby? I'm here at your poor car."

Clay held up the keys. "She dropped these."

"Clay found your keys laying in the road." She nodded her thanks to Clay. "Right. Okay. I'll see you soon."

21

Yvette held her hand out, taking the keys. "Turns out my airhead sister forgot to grab her suitcase before she went tooling off with Wanda." She eyed Clay. "I guess she was still distracted."

"I have that effect on some people."

"No, just Abby." Yvette opened the back hatch, peered in, and sighed. "Now I need to find a way to transfer all her crap into my Mustang before we can get this towed to the shop."

Clay scanned the contents. Three suitcases, pillows, a computer bag, and a variety of boxes were stacked up to nearly the roof of the vehicle. "It's a miracle she didn't hit someone sooner. How could she possibly see through all that stuff?"

"Backup camera?" Yvette asked. Then she shook her head. "Doesn't matter. Not even half that stuff will fit in my car."

"Don't worry about it," Clay said. "I have to drop some brew samples off at the house for Lin. I can load this stuff in my Jeep and haul it over."

"You don't have to do that," Yvette said, eyeing him with suspicion.

"I know. I don't mind. It's not a big deal," he said. Of course it was a big deal. He'd just lied about bringing Lin some beer samples, all because the only thing he could think about in that moment was seeing Abigail again. He took the keys back from Yvette. "Tell her I'll bring everything by in a few hours when I get off work."

Yvette snorted. "Sure. Just remember, she not staying."

He eyed the contents of the car. "You could've fooled me."

CHAPTER 4

"Y ou need a beer," Wanda announced as she took a right at the end of Main Street, leaving behind Clay and the rest of the town.

"You can say that again." Abby rubbed a hand over the back of her neck, praying she didn't wake up the next morning with a severe case of whiplash. She hadn't been going that fast had she? *Fast enough.* She hadn't even pumped the brakes before running into the teenager's car. "Hey, who do you know that drives a Mini Cooper? A white one?"

Wanda pursed her lips as she concentrated. "Here in town?"

"Yeah. The girl I hit said she was driving her aunt's car without permission. I'd really like to find out who the car belongs to so I can apologize and make sure she has my insurance info."

"Hmm. I can't recall anyone off the top of my head, but if I think of someone I'll let you know." Wanda veered the cart to the left, steering it onto the special golf-cart-only path the town had put in specifically for the large population of golf cart riders. To the left was a large grassy grove, and to the right was the Keating Hollow magical wish-casting brook, sparkling in the late afternoon sun. It wasn't unusual to see witches using the waters to enhance their spells. Today was no different. A dark-skinned woman stood in the middle of the brook, her arms held high, her face tilted to the sun as her lips moved in a chant.

Once again, that sense of peace washed over Abby, her heart and soul content to be *home*. She let out a sigh, even as the all too familiar unease and guilt started to creep in.

"Someone needs libations," Wanda announced as she pulled over to the side of the path. She gave Abby a conspiratorial grin, jumped out of the driver's seat, and headed for the back of the golf cart.

"What are you—?" Abby started.

"What's your poison?" Wanda waved for Abby to join her as she lifted the back seat on the golf cart. "Chocolate Stout? Pumpkin Spice Ale? Or if you really want to get crazy, I have Caramel Fest Porter."

Abby stared down into the cooler and recognized the Keating Hollow Brewery label. Then she laughed, shaking her head. "Since when does Dad make flavored beers?"

"Since Clay Garrison became his master brewer."

Abby took a step back and blinked. "Clay is the master brewer?"

"Sure." Wanda tilted her head to the side and studied Abby with a look of concern. "You didn't know?"

"No. When did that happen?" If Clay was already bottling new brews, he had to have been promoted to brew master at least a month or more ago. Why hadn't anyone told her? She'd admit, she'd been slightly out of touch with her family, but it wasn't like she ever ignored their calls. And she'd spoken to or texted with Yvette at least a half dozen times over the last few months.

Wanda frowned. "Uh, I'm not sure exactly. But the last time I was in there Lin did say Clay's been his right hand man since West left for culinary school last year."

"West left for culinary school?" Abby gaped at her friend. The tall, linebacker-sized man wore a long beard and had spent his entire high school career working at his father's restoration shop, grease covering him from head to toe. Imagining him whipping up delicate sauces and amuse-bouches amused her to no end. But again, why hadn't anyone filled her in? Last she could recall, her dad had said West moved to Napa to be with his longtime girlfriend.

"You really need a refreshing on town gossip, don't you?"

"It appears so," Abby said, wondering what else she'd missed over the last ten years. "How did West get into cooking?"

Wanda snorted. "Vegas trip. Something about a hook-up with the assistant on the Magical Chef. You know, that cooking show that airs on the Spellbound channel. The next thing we knew, he was obsessed with cooking. He makes these crab phyllo tarts that are to *die* for."

Abby's stomach rumbled just as "House of the Rising Sun" started playing on her phone. A wave of anxiety hit her. She was not in the mood to talk to her on-again, off-again boyfriend right after running into Clay. They were currently in an off-again phase, but ever since she'd told him she was returning to Keating Hollow, he'd been acting as if everything between them was perfectly fine.

"You gonna answer that?" Wanda asked, eyeing Abby.

Abby nodded and glanced down at Logan's handsome face flashing on the screen, his blue eyes downcast as he concentrated on one of his moody New Orleans paintings. It was her favorite picture of him, but instead of bringing her joy, all it did was make her frustrated. When they'd met two years ago, he'd been an artist who very much lived his life on his own terms—a total free spirit. But six months ago he'd tossed aside his paintbrushes and gone to work for his father's real estate development company. Now all he talked about were permits, city council meetings, and profits.

"Abby? Where are you?" Logan's voice sounded rushed, and there was a rustling noise over the connection.

"Keating Hollow. I just got into town about thirty minutes ago. I was going to call—"

"Good. That's good. Glad you made it safely. How's your dad?" A door slammed, followed by a familiar dog barking in the background.

"I don't know. I haven't seen him yet." She frowned. "Where are you?"

"I just left your place. I had to pick up some painting supplies I left here after the store closed."

"You're painting again?" Abby asked, genuinely happy for him. He was so talented. It killed her that he'd all but given up after his art gallery had gone under eight months ago.

"Me?" He let out a humorless laugh. "No. There's no time for that right now. The daughter of one of the partners is interested in learning, so I was roped into giving her a lesson. You wouldn't believe this a-hole, Abs. He thinks painting is a fun hobby. And now I have to spend my one day off teaching some novice how to paint something other than a straight line."

Her joy fled, and disappointment for him weighed on her heart. Still, there was a bright side. "At least you'll get a paintbrush in your hand. It could be worse."

He let out a *humph*. "You know I'm not any good at giving lessons, especially to beginners. It's too bad you aren't here. You'd be perfect, considering you're still in the learning phase yourself. All those classes you took would finally come in handy."

All of her concern for his artistic pursuits fled, and a ball of indignation formed in her gut as Abby bit back a snarky reply. 'Still in the learning phase.' What the hell did that mean? Abby had been painting since she'd left Keating Hollow ten years ago. And yeah, she'd taken a bunch of classes and still did when she had time. She liked to explore different techniques and approaches. As far as she was concerned, she'd always be learning. The comment itself didn't necessarily irritate her. It was the meaning behind it. In Logan's mind, he was an award-winning, accomplished painter, while Abby was little better than a hobbyist. Never mind that she made a living off her paintings and handmade soaps at the art market. But her work wasn't hanging in a gallery, so clearly she wasn't accomplished in his estimation.

"Abs?" he asked when she didn't respond.

"I'm here." She stared at the tranquil brook, wondering what effect the magical properties of the water would have on her healing lotions.

"Anyway, I called to ask if you think you'll be back in New Orleans by the twenty-first."

"Of this month?" Abby asked. "That's like two-and-a-half weeks."

"Right. But there's this dinner meeting with some investors, and one of them requested your presence. I think it might mean the difference between him funding this project or not."

Of course that's why he'd called. Everything was all about him these days. Abby gritted her teeth and swallowed a huff of irritation. "I'm sorry, Logan, but I doubt it. I already told you that depending on how things are, I might be here through the holidays."

"Right. Right. But if I got you a plane ticket, do you think you could come home for a few days?"

She tightened her fingers around the phone. "Can we talk about this later? I haven't even seen my family yet."

"Of course. It's just that…"

"Just that what?" She was all out of patience. Did he really expect her to drive more than halfway across the country and then turn around and fly back just to schmooze an investor for a development deal for his father? She had much bigger issues to deal with at the moment.

"The meeting is important. I *need* you here. You said if I took this job for my father that you'd be supportive."

That was before he'd decided they needed a 'break.' Abby pulled the phone away from her ear, stared at it in disbelief, and then shook her head in exasperation.

"Abby," he said. "You still there?"

"I'm here," she said, wondering when he'd turned into such a selfish a-hole. "I just can't make any decisions until I see my dad."

"Well, think about it, okay? The dinner meeting is at that restaurant you said you wanted to try—August in the business district. I bet the flight would be worth it just for the duck."

Abby didn't respond. What would she say? That she couldn't give two flying pigs about the restaurant and that there was no way on the goddess's green earth that she would be there? She didn't have the energy to deal with Logan's guilt trip and certainly not in front of Wanda. Ever since Logan's art gallery closed, he'd changed in small ways. Instead of the easygoing artist who had charmed her with his art, he now spent most of his time on the phone, in front of a computer, or at business meetings that all too often ended up at the strip clubs. It wasn't what she'd signed up for. Still, out of some sense of loyalty and friendship, she'd supported his decision and had been his plus-one more often than not. But right now, she needed to focus on her family.

"I'll call you tomorrow, okay?" he said.

"Sure. Tomorrow." Her voice sounded flat to her own ears and she cringed, not wanting to create a rift between them when she was two thousand miles away.

"Hey, Abs?" Logan said, his voice suddenly soft and full of concern.

"Yeah?"

"Don't worry until there's something to worry about, okay? No use borrowing trouble."

It was what her dad used to always say when she was a kid. "You're right. Thanks for that."

"I'm glad you're home. It's where you need to be," he added.

"Really?" That wasn't the impression he'd given when he'd been asking her to come right back to New Orleans.

"Of course. As much as I'd like you to be here, I know you have to do this for you and your family. I didn't mean for it to sound like I didn't get that. I do. And if it works out you can come back for a few days, great. If not, I get it and I'll survive... somehow." There was humor in his tone now, and she found her lips curving into a ghost of a smile.

"I'll see how it goes. In the meantime, I'm sure Lily can rescue you from being dateless to any scary business dinners."

Logan snorted. "I think I'd rather take crazy Aunt Polly. At least she wouldn't tell them to stop their dick-waving."

Abby laughed. The one time they'd run into her roommate while at one of the insufferable meetings, Logan had asked her to join them. Within five minutes, two of the investors had hit on her, then in a stroke of idiocy, started discussing who had the bigger real estate portfolio, as if that would impress her. She'd stood up, announced she wasn't interested in the size of any of their assets, accused them of shameless dick-waving, and left before her dinner had even arrived. "I hope they like the smell of patchouli oil."

Chuckling, he said, "How is it possible Aunt Polly and my father are from the same parents?"

"It's one of those cosmic questions that will forever remain unanswered."

"You've got that right."

Silence fell between them for a moment until Abby cleared her throat. "I better go. I'll call you tomorrow."

"Abs?"

"Yeah?"

"That thing I said about us taking a break?"

"Forget it, Logan. We'll talk about it later," she said, seriously tired and in no mood to rehash their relationship status.

"It's just that I wanted to say I was wrong. I think I was stressed, but now that you're not here... damn. You've only been gone for three days, and I'm a mess." He chuckled softly. "Stupid, right? Anyway, forget what I said about a break. I miss you... I—I love you, Abby. When you get home I think we should move in together."

Abigail blinked, staring at nothing as shock reverberated through her. Had she heard him right? Had he just uttered the word love for the first time in their two-year relationship over the phone? And ask her to move in with him? She tried to respond, but the words got caught in her throat and all that came out was an annoying squeak. She cleared her throat. "I... um..."

"Abby, didn't you just hear me? I said I love you."

"I heard," she said softly. "I just wasn't expecting that. I think I'm overwhelmed. The long drive, and my dad, and everything. I'm not sure what to say."

"You could just say you love me too," he said, sounding irritated.

"Right. I—me, too, Logan. We'll talk about moving in together later, okay? I have to go. My ride is waiting." *Me, too.* Was that even true? Did she love him? At one point, she'd thought she did, but what did it mean that she couldn't say the words?

There was a long, pregnant pause. Then he let out a sigh and said, "Okay, Abby. I'll call you tomorrow."

"Okay. Goodnight, Logan."

The phone line disconnected without Logan saying another word. Abby closed her eyes, mentally exhausted. After taking a deep breath, she turned to find Wanda watching her.

"The boyfriend?" Wanda asked.

"Sort of... We're kind of on a break. His name's Logan."

She arched one eyebrow. "I didn't intend to eavesdrop but… it sounds like someone's finding out what it means to be on his own and he's not happy about it."

Abby shrugged. "He's got a lot going on, and apparently he's having a bit of trouble adjusting to me being out of town."

"Humph. Well, he's a big boy, he'll figure it out."

"No doubt." Abby reached down into the golf cart's cooler and grabbed a chocolate stout.

Without a word, Wanda handed her a bottle opener then fished out a bottle of the Caramel Fest Porter. She held it up in a salute. "Thank the powers that be for the special golf cart path, where beer flows just as freely as the river."

Abby snickered and climbed back into the cart. When Wanda joined her, Abby asked, "How fast does this thing go?"

With a wicked gleam, Wanda pressed her foot all the way down on the pedal and said, "There's only one way to find out."

CHAPTER 5

"*D*ad?" Abigail called, her spirits lifted after Wanda finished the drive to the house in a hilarious series of golf cart donuts out in the circular driveway. She strolled through the redwood log cabin and let out a sigh of contentment as she gazed out the floor-to-ceiling windows at the view of three hundred rolling acres of the Alchemy River Valley. The Townsends had been the first family to settle in the valley that was surrounded by a glorious redwood forest over a century ago. And no matter how far she ran, there was no escaping the deep roots she always felt when she was home.

At that moment, she thought she'd be content to stay forever. But she knew that within a few days, her flight reflex would kick in and she'd be plotting how to get out of dodge. Maybe she *should* consider going back to New Orleans for a few days. It wasn't like she'd be gone long.

She tucked the thought into the back of her mind and walked through the living room, noting that nothing had changed since her last visit. Not the worn leather sectional couch, the old rocking chair that creaked every time it moved, nor the impressive amount of beeswax candles covering practically every spare surface. Even the wrought iron pentacle her father had hung over the stone fire place on her eighth birthday—the day after her mother had left them—was still in place.

A sharp pain sliced through her as if a scab had just been ripped off, revealing an old festering wound. Dammit. Would she ever get over her mother's selfish abandonment? Considering it'd been twenty years since she'd watched her mother's old Volvo disappear down the street for the last time, she highly doubted she'd find peace any time soon.

Abigail crossed the threshold into the glass sunporch and instantly felt better. Outside, her father's yard was as glorious as ever. Three different varieties of berry bushes filled one side of the clearing, while an apple orchard covered the other. Right in the middle was her father's private vegetable garden. If she knew her father, he'd planted every kind of winter vegetable imaginable plus a few summer varieties only he could manage to grow in such a cool climate.

Her fingers itched to touch the dirt, to help weed the beds, to connect with the soft earth. The magic inside her swelled to overwhelming levels, and she made herself take a step back. This was her father's domain. Not hers. She cast a glance to the east of the garden and spotted the pretty little studio her father had built for her and quickly averted her eyes. There were too many memories locked in those walls. Memories she wasn't ready to face.

"Abby!" a cheerful voice called from behind her. "You're here!"

Abby spun, her heart swelling as she smiled at her sister, Faith. The waif-thin blonde was the youngest of the four Townsend sisters. And even though she'd just turned twenty-five, she didn't look a day over eighteen in her faded jeans, long-sleeved dragon T-shirt, and sheepskin Ugg boots.

Faith launched herself at her sister, her long, wavy blond hair flying out behind her. She hugged Abby with such force, Abby found it hard to breathe. "Whoa," she said. "Don't bruise a rib, okay?"

"Sorry," Faith said with a chuckle. "It's just been so long since you've been home."

Abby pulled back and smoothed her T-shirt. "I just saw you a few months ago when you came to New Orleans."

Faith tsked. "It was nine months ago, and we were so busy, I barely saw you at all."

"That's not true. What about that night we went to dinner and then the jazz club on Frenchmen Street? Plus, you hung out with me at the Art Market and helped me package a bunch of soap I'd finished."

"Fine, I saw you, but we certainly didn't get any time to catch up. Do you recall one conversation that didn't revolve around work or how to save Logan's art gallery?"

Abby winced, recalling how crazed she'd been, trying to keep everything together. "I'm sorry, Faith. You're right. I guess I was pretty selfish, wasn't I?"

"No, that's not what I meant at all," her sister said, shaking her head. "You had stuff to deal with. We all do. I just meant we didn't really get the quality time I'd hoped for. Please tell me you're home for more than just a few days."

A ball of unease formed in the pit of Abigail's stomach as she nodded, confirming her intention to stay in town. Goddess, why was that so hard? She loved her family. Loved the town. She just couldn't escape the crushing regret and the reasons she'd left in the first place. "I'll be here. Just need to find a place to rent so I can fill my soap orders."

Faith gave her an impatient look. "You know you can make

your soaps here in your studio, Abs. Dad won't let anyone else in there. Says it's your domain."

"No, I don't think so," Abby said stubbornly. "You know I can't work in there. I'll find somewhere else. Surely someone can spare some space. All I need is running water and power. I can work out everything else."

"Whatever." Faith shook her head, her expression more sad than annoyed. "Just as long as you don't skip town while we still need you here."

"Now you sound like Yvette."

"Good," Yvette said from behind them. "Maybe someone else can get through to her. Goddess knows my methods aren't working."

Abby and Faith both turned to find the oldest of the Townsend sisters leaning against the doorframe between the living room and the sun porch. Her hair was pulled back into a neat pony tail, her makeup flawless, and except for her soot-smudged jeans, no one would've ever guessed she'd just spent the last few hours dealing with a forest fire.

"It's nice to see you, too, Yvette," Abby said and moved in to give her sister a quick hug. But Yvette wrapped her arms around her and held on, holding her in place for a long moment. When she finally let go and Abby pulled away, Yvette's eyes were damp as she blinked away her tears.

Abby's world suddenly came crashing down around her, and she couldn't stop her own tears as they fell unchecked down her cheeks.

Yvette grabbed Abby and Faith's hands and squeezed. "I'm so glad you're here, Abs."

"Me, too," Faith said, grabbing Abby's free hand. The three of them stood together in a small circle, no one speaking as they fought the well of emotion threatening to undo them all.

Finally Abby pulled free, and in a shaky tone she asked, "Where's Dad?"

"He's in the orchard with Isaac, inspecting the trees for fungus," Yvette said. "They should be in soon."

"How is Isaac?" Abby asked, referring to her sister's husband of twelve years. They'd married when Yvette was just twenty-one and to hear Yvette tell it, he was the perfect husband. He helped Dad with the farm, cleaned house, walked the dog, did the accounting for Yvette's book store, and managed his own online magical gaming business without complaint. They were the all-American couple. All that was missing were the two point three kids.

"Good," she said, but Abby didn't miss the way she glanced away or the tightening of her tone as she spoke. "Same." Then Yvette glanced up and peered at Abby. "What about you? How's Logan?"

Abby sighed. "Fine, I guess."

"Fine, you guess?" Yvette said with a sad chuckle. "That's reassuring."

"He's been weird ever since the gallery closed. We're on a break." Abby plunked at the hem of her shirt. "I don't really want to talk about it."

"How about we head to the kitchen," Faith said, tugging their hands. "We can make hot cocoa and talk about Clay instead."

"Right," Yvette said with a smirk. "But if we're gonna talk about Clay, Abby might need something a little stronger."

"The only thing we need to talk about is why no one told me he's now the master brewer at the brewery," Abby said as she climbed up on one of the barstools.

Both of her sisters turned and stared at her.

"What?"

"Dad didn't tell you?" Yvette asked.

Abby placed both hands on the polished wood counter. "Nope. Wanda did. She was kind enough to give me a ride after I rear-ended some poor girl driving a Mini Cooper."

"You got into an accident? Today?" Faith gasped out. "Are you all right?"

"I'm fine." Abby waved a dismissive hand. "My car, on the other hand, isn't. I'm going to need to get it towed to the shop sooner rather than later. It's parked on Main Street with its front end all smashed in."

"I bet Clay takes care of it after he unloads your stuff," Yvette said.

Abby turned to stare at her older sister. "*Clay* is going to unload my stuff?"

"Sure." Yvette climbed onto one of the kitchen counter stools. "He said he needed to come by the house to give Dad something tonight, so he offered to haul your stuff over while he was at it. I would've done it after I talked to you, but there was no way all that stuff was going to fit into my tiny car."

Abby groaned. The last thing she wanted was for her ex-boyfriend to be handling all her stuff. What if he...? Oh, goddess. She closed her eyes and shook her head as she remembered the canvas bag she'd stuffed full of her lacy bras and panties. The bag didn't even have a zipper. Without a doubt, he was once again going to get a peek at her unmentionables.

Yvette snickered. "So... I'm guessing the reunion was interesting. Tell us everything."

"Yeah. What'd he say?" Faith leaned in, placing her forearms on the counter.

"Uh... nothing." Heat burned Abigail's face as she recalled the sparks that had crackled between them.

"Riiiight." Yvette twisted her long sun-kissed chestnut locks up into a knot on the top of her head and slipped off the stool.

She crossed the large kitchen, reached into the stainless steel double-wide refrigerator, then pulled out a bottle of Irish cream, and held it up. "Looks like we're going to need to prime the pump if we want any dirt, Faith."

"I'm on it." Faith grabbed the bottle and started rummaging around in the cabinet. Yvette moved in to help and in no time, there was a mug of Irish cream-spiked hot cocoa topped with whipped cream sitting in front of Abigail.

Faith raised her mug and said, "Drink up."

Yvette followed suit, and Abigail lifted her mug, clinking it with her sisters'. After taking a long sip, her eyes widened. "Mother earth. Is this made with melted chocolate? It's delicious."

Faith nodded. "There's plenty more where that came from."

"I bet," Abigail said as the room spun slightly. She set the mug down on the counter, wondering if a one bottle of beer and a quarter cup of Irish cocoa could really make her head spin. She got to her feet and had to hold onto the counter to steady herself. "What did you do to that drink?"

Faith frowned. "Nothing special." She took a small sip of her own drink. "It's not even that strong."

"When's the last time you ate anything?" Yvette studied her sister then slapped her hand over her mouth as she let out a little gasp. "You're not pregnant are you?"

"What? No," Abby said, annoyed.

"Are you sure? You look really pale all of a sudden. Are you going to pass out?" Yvette wrapped an arm around Abby's waist. "Lean on me."

"I'm fine. Really. I just need something to eat." Abby stepped away from her sister and grabbed a cookie from the nearby cookie jar. She bit into the buttery shortbread and moaned. "Oh, man alive, who made these?"

"Noel," Faith said. "She keeps Dad stocked."

Abigail swallowed her mouthful of cookie. "Where is Noel? Is she coming by?"

Yvette and Faith shared a glance, and then both of them shrugged. "Not sure," Faith said. "She was... noncommittal."

Of course, Abby thought. Her relationship with Noel had started to deteriorate the day Abby had left town ten years ago. Time had only made it worse. Abby tried—goddess knew, she'd tried. The first couple of years, Abby had texted, called, emailed, sent birthday cards, and had even purchased a ticket to come home to be present for the birth of her only niece, but Noel simply wouldn't respond. She'd frozen Abigail out of her life and told her in no uncertain terms to back off.

Abby had finally taken the hint. She no longer called or texted Noel, but she did Facetime and send regular cards and birthday gifts to Daisy, Noel's six-year-old. "I expected as much," Abby said and sat back down on the stool.

No one said anything for a moment, but then Faith jumped to her feet and moved to the fridge. "You need something more than a cookie."

"Is there pie?" Abby asked.

"Of course there is," Faith scoffed.

"It wouldn't be the Townsend household if there wasn't pie," Yvette chimed in.

"Blackberry or Apple?" Faith asked.

"Both," Yvette and Abby said at the same time and then laughed.

"Both it is." Faith pulled out the pie tins and homemade whipped cream, while Yvette made a fresh pot of coffee.

The three sisters were just about done eating when they heard the front door open again. Abby put her fork down and slipped off her stool, expecting to finally see her father. But instead, the sound of young feet echoed through the house, and a second later, a small dark-haired girl ran into the kitchen calling, "Aunt Abby!"

Abby grinned and squatted down, her arms held out wide. The little girl flung herself into Abby's arms and as Abby hugged her tightly, her heart swelled with so much love she thought the organ might burst. "It's so good to see you, little girl," Abby whispered.

Daisy squirmed out of her aunt's arms. "I'm not little anymore, Auntie. Mommy said I grew two inches and I'm a big girl now."

"Two inches? Wow. I'm impressed." Abby leaned in and gave her a loud kiss on her cheek. "I guess your mommy's right." Abby glanced up and spotted Noel standing in the kitchen threshold, her arms crossed over her chest. She'd dyed her hair bright red and cut it into an asymmetrical bob. Sleek and gorgeous, Abby thought as she smiled at her sister, but Noel just stared at her then turned and walked back into the living room.

Ouch.

It appeared some wounds never healed. At least Noel hadn't tried to keep Daisy from knowing or loving her aunt. Not that Abby had expected her to. That wasn't Noel's style. The woman was stubborn, but not cruel.

"She'll come around," Faith said.

"I doubt it." Yvette shoved the last of her pie in her mouth then washed it down with a gulp of coffee. Holding her hand out to Daisy, she said, "Come on, sweetie. Grandpa has a surprise for you."

Daisy slipped her small hand into Yvette's, and the pair of them disappeared outside.

Another set of footsteps caught Abigail's attention, and she glanced up to find a radiant woman with dark skin and a warm smile.

"Abby!" Hanna beamed and wrapped her arms around Abigail, giving her a hug. She held on tightly and said, "It's so good to see you."

"You, too," Abigail forced out around the lump in her throat. Hanna was Abigail's best friend's little sister and a near clone of Charlotte, too. Hanna was a smidge taller than Charlotte had been, and her eyes were slightly more wideset, but when Charlotte had still been alive, most people had mistaken them for twins.

Abigail stepped back and took a good look at Hanna. She wore a long knit sweater over a flowy peasant blouse, skinny jeans, and chic, steel blue, knee-high boots. The young woman looked like she'd just stepped off the pages of magazine. "You look gorgeous."

"Me?" Hanna waved a dismissive hand. "This is all Noel's handiwork. We just got done finishing a photoshoot. If you'd caught me on any other day, you'd have found my hair in a bun and me wearing ripped jeans and a sweatshirt."

"That's the Hanna I remember." Abby gave her a wistful smile then studied her spiked cocoa as memories of Charlotte started to flicker through her mind.

"Hey." Hanna reached out and grabbed Abby's hand.

Abby stared down at the connection, her heart aching for Charlotte and her own failure to save the life of the girl who'd been the best friend she'd ever had.

Hanna squeezed Abby's hand and said, "My parents would really love to see you while you're home."

Abby's head snapped up, panic clawing at her chest. She stiffened and forced herself to breathe. After a moment, she gave a noncommittal shrug. "I'm not sure how long I'll be home, but I'll try."

"They miss you, you know."

Tears burned the backs of Abigail's eyes again, and she

turned away, blinking rapidly to get herself under control. "I miss them, too, Hanna. I'll try. I promise."

Hanna let out a quiet sigh, and Abby winced. She'd promised Hanna she'd go see the Pelshes before, but she'd never followed through. And she knew in her heart she wouldn't this time either.

Shame washed over her and she turned to apologize, but Hanna had disappeared, somehow managing to silently slip from the kitchen to somewhere else in the rambling house.

CHAPTER 6

*C*lay steered his six-year-old Jeep down the mile-long, tree-lined drive that led to the Townsend family home. It was the same as it always was; the trees perfectly manicured, the road well maintained, and twinkle lights wrapped around the periodic gas-lit lamp poles.

Nostalgia washed over him, and a deep ache settled in his bones as his thoughts turned to Abby, the girl he'd loved with everything he had all through high school. The one he'd thought he was going to marry and would be the mother of his children someday. The ache intensified and nearly took his breath away.

"Stupid," he muttered and tightened his grip on the steering wheel. He'd been so naïve back then, believing that love would conquer all and that nothing could tear them apart. Now he knew better, knew that romanticizing what might have been was a complete waste of time. Abby had made her choices and so had he. Now they barely knew one another.

Well, he knew one thing; she still wore those sexy lace bras that had driven him out of his mind at the tender age of eighteen. What he wouldn't do to see her in one of those now. Picturing her creamy, full breasts popping out over the lace was enough to drive him to madness.

"Hell," he said as he lowered his window, letting the coastal air cool down his heated skin. "Get a grip, Clay." Whatever he'd had with Abby was long gone, and reminiscing about their youth wasn't going to solve any of his problems. Besides, even if there was something there, he was certain she'd never stay in Keating Hollow. And that was a deal breaker. He wouldn't put himself through that again, not when he had Olive to consider. He couldn't get involved with anyone who wouldn't be a stable force in his daughter's life.

No. No matter how much he wanted Abby, even after all these years, she was strictly off-limits.

Too bad he'd already gone out of his way to make sure he saw her again today.

The house came into view, and he wasn't sure if he was annoyed or relieved to see the line of cars parked in the drive. No doubt the entire family was already there. At least they'd act as a buffer if he let his libido get out of control. Who could blame him after he'd accidentally spotted that rich purple thong in her open bag?

The front door swung open just as he put his Jeep into park, and Faith stepped out onto the front porch. The sun glinted off her golden hair, casting a halo glow around her.

Fitting, Clay thought. Of the four sisters, Faith was the sweetest. Thoughtful and soft spoken, she was the one who was always there for anyone who needed someone to talk to. Hell, she'd been there for him on more than one occasion after Abby had left and again when he'd returned home after his marriage imploded. He climbed out of his Jeep holding three growlers and made his way up the house.

"I hear you have some new samples for us," Faith said.

"Right here. Caramel Chocolate Malt, Fall Spice, and Toffee Java."

Faith rubbed her hands together. "Toffee Java! You took my suggestion."

Clay gave her a sly smile. "Sure did. And just between us, it's my new favorite. But don't tell your pops. I want him to form his own opinions."

She laughed. "Like Dad has ever let anyone sway his opinion when it comes to beer."

Clay grinned. She had a point. Lin Townsend was a man of strong opinions when it came to his business, and especially his beer. But Clay had witnessed him form opinions based on what his daughters thought on more than one occasion, even if they didn't realize it.

"Come on," she said, taking the growlers. "Everyone's inside."

But Clay shook his head. "I can't really stay. There's somewhere I need to be in about a half hour," he lied. "I'll just unload Abby's stuff so I can get back to town."

"That's too bad." Faith frowned. "We were having spiked cocoa and pie."

"Tempting, but I really can't stay. Maybe next time."

She eyed him, suspicion written all over her angelic face. She was on to him. She knew he was making up excuses just so he didn't get sucked into the Townsend family reunion. What had he been thinking?

The door swung open, and Abby stepped out onto the porch, her cheeks slightly rosy and her eyes bright. There was a small smile claiming her lips, and she looked so lovely it was all he could do to stay rooted to his spot and not sweep her up in his arms and carry her off back to his place.

"Clay," she said, glancing between him and his Jeep. "You

really didn't have to go to all the trouble of bringing me my stuff.

He cleared his throat. "It was no big deal. I was stopping by anyway."

Faith snorted a laugh.

"Faith," Abby said, a warning in her tone.

"Yes?" Faith answered, all innocence.

"Why don't you go inside where you can mind your own business."

Her younger sister laughed, wiggled her fingers at Clay, and disappeared back into the house with the beer samples.

"Sorry about that." Abby jumped down off the porch and strolled past Clay to the back of the Jeep.

He watched her, his eyes automatically focusing on her shapely backside. *Damn*, he thought. She was even lovelier than she'd been at eighteen. His insides tightened, and he forced himself to glance away.

"This was really sweet of you," she said as she lifted the hatchback. "I don't know what I was thinking taking off with Wanda without even grabbing my suitcase."

Clay shrugged. "I imagine you were just anxious to see your dad. How is he today?"

She grabbed her canvas bag, the one full of her lingerie, and glanced over at him. "Good I guess. He's been out in the orchard ever since I got in. He'll probably be in soon. You can wait for him inside while I unload this stuff."

His gaze travelled over her face, noting her tired expression and the faint circles under her eyes. She was exhausted after driving all the way from New Orleans on her own. He shook his head. "No, it's okay. I'll help you unload."

"You really don't—"

Clay held up his hand. "I know I don't have to, Abs. But I want to, okay?"

She glanced away, but not before he noticed the emotion rolling through her clear blue eyes. She'd never been one who could hide what she was feeling, and that hadn't changed. Was she that worried about her dad, or was it something else?

"All right. Most of this stuff can just go in the garage for now." She walked over to her dad's truck and reached in, pressing the garage door opener.

"You got it." While Abby pulled out her travel bags, Clay started moving her boxes of supplies into the garage. But as he picked up a container of glass jars, he frowned. "Don't you want this stuff in your studio?"

"No. The garage is fine."

"It's not a big deal. I can just drive it over there—"

"Clay, it's fine," she said, her body stiff and her face blank.

He knew that look. He'd seen it more times than he could count. It meant she had her hackles up, and no matter what he said she wouldn't back down. Stubborn didn't begin to describe her when she was dead set against something. "Can I ask why? Aren't you going to be working over there?"

She shook her head, clutching one of her canvas bags to her body.

"I see." He glanced from the pile of supplies in the garage to the little studio on the edge of the property. "Does anyone use it these days?"

She shook her head again and let out an audible sigh.

"That's a shame." He watched the fire inside her flame out and turn to weariness as she turned her attention back to unloading the Jeep. Everything about her screamed exhaustion. "Here. I can get that." Clay reached out to the take the open bag from her, but she sidestepped him, hauling the heavy bag out of the Jeep. She backed up, misjudged where she'd left her other suitcases, and stumbled over the pile of luggage. Time stopped, and almost as if in slow motion, the bag she was holding tumbled out of the Jeep, its contents floating through the late afternoon air and scattering all over the drive.

Clay was speechless as he took in the scene. The bag just happened to be her lingerie bag, and pink, black, red, green, and purple lace covered the concrete, appearing as if Victoria's Secret had exploded in the Townsend driveway.

Abby let out a gasp and scrambled to grab her bras and panties while Clay chuckled.

"Need some help with that?" he asked, rocking back on his heels, completely amused.

"No." She sent him an annoyed glance as she frantically stuffed her panties back into the bag.

"It's really no problem. I mean, it's nothing I haven't handled before."

She rolled her eyes and stood up, hands on her hips, trying to act as if she was unaffected by the incident. But her face was bright red and she had trouble looking him in the eye. "Funny. Can we just pretend this never happened?"

"I don't think so, Abs. It's going to be next to impossible to forget seeing you stuff your underwear into your bag just like you used to when we'd get caught making out in your shed." The words flew out of his mouth before he could stop them. But it was worth it when her face turned a deeper shade of red and her mouth worked, unable to form words. He laughed, enjoying watching her flustered. Leaning in, he whispered, "Don't worry, Abby. Your secrets are safe with me."

Winking, he grabbed another box and carried it to the garage. When he turned around, all traces of her were gone, except for a sliver of red poking out from under the Jeep. He reached down and picked up the forgotten panties, the lace so soft it felt like velvet.

"Good goddess," he muttered as his entire body heated.

"Clay?" Lin's deep voice reverberated from behind him.

Clay quickly shoved the lace into his pocket and turned around, hoping he didn't look as guilty as he felt. Hell, what was he, seventeen again? It wasn't like he was doing anything other than helping Abby unload the car... unless one counted picturing her naked with her bra and underwear on the floor. He cleared his throat. "Lin, how are you doing?"

"Good." The older man nodded to the car and raised an eyebrow. "You moving in?"

"Not today, but it's good to know it's an option." Clay grinned at the older man.

"I wouldn't say I'm offering, but if you were in dire straits, we could probably find room for you in the shed."

Clay laughed. "Thanks. I'm just dropping off Abby's things. After the accident today—"

"Accident?" Lin's gaze scanned the driveway then landed on the front door as Abby came striding back out.

"Dad!" Abby's entire face lit up as she spotted her father and ran from the porch, her arms out.

Lin caught her in a giant bear hug, lifting her right off her feet. "Welcome home, Abby-girl." He held her there, suspended off the ground for a few moments before carefully placing her back onto her feet. Then he studied her closely. "Are you okay? Nothing bruised or broken?"

"Fine time to ask me that now that you've squeezed the air right out of me." She rubbed her palm over her chest and quickly added, "I'm fine. Just a fender-bender."

Lin glanced over at Clay, clearly looking for confirmation.

"No one was hurt," Clay confirmed. "There's a Mini Cooper running around town with a smashed back end, and Abby's car is going to need a makeover, but otherwise it appears both parties escaped unscathed."

"Dad," Abby said, her hands once again on her hips. "I don't need Clay to speak for me."

"Of course you don't," he agreed with a shake of his head. "But I do need him to vouch for you. If you're anything like your sisters, ever since we learned of the cancer, no one wants to upset me. I've learned if I want the truth, I need to find corroborating witnesses."

"Oh, for the love of Tink," she said, rolling her eyes as she slipped her arm around his waist and leaned in for another sideways hug. "How about this? I promise to always tell you the brutal truth as long as you promise to not leave me in the dark." She glanced at Clay pointedly. "Like not telling me when you hand over the brew master duties to someone else."

Her father cast a sideways glance at Clay then turned back to her, nodding. "Deal." He held out his hand, but Abby ignored it and hugged him tighter instead. She whispered something that Clay couldn't hear, and her father tightened his hold on her for just a second before letting her go.

"There. Now I have to finish unloading this stuff. What are you up to?" Abby asked him.

"Need to talk to Clay for a minute about the samples he brought over then I'll be inside."

"Okay, there's a mug of spiked hot cocoa with your name on it." She smiled at her dad, grabbed another couple bags, and hurried back inside.

Lin turned to Clay, his eyebrows raised. "What are you really doing here, Clay?"

Busted. Clay had never brought Lin samples of the brews before. Even though Lin had backed off the operations at the brewery, he still came in at least three times a week. Chances were he'd be in the very next day. "Just helping your daughter out."

Lin pursed his lips. "I can see that. You know she has someone back in New Orleans, right?"

A familiar dull ache formed just above his heart, and he unconsciously rubbed at his chest as he shook his head. "No, I didn't. But that's not why I'm here."

"Isn't it, though?" Lin asked, staring him down with his steely gray eyes.

Dammit. He couldn't lie to the old man. It was obvious he was seeing right through him. Clay sucked in a breath and blew it out. "You don't have anything to worry about, Lin. I'm not interested in getting in the middle of anything. You don't have to worry about her."

Lin moved in closer and lowered his voice. "It's not Abby I'm worried about, son. I love my daughter, and the gods know she's got a smart head on her shoulders with that business of hers she runs. But when it comes to matters of the heart, she hasn't quite figured things out. If you're going to let her back into your life, just be careful. You hear what I'm saying?"

Clay stared at his boss, at a loss for words. Lin's frankness was appreciated, but at the same time, he was offended on Abby's behalf. She was a grown woman, after all, and deserved to make her decisions free of judgment, even from her father. Finally, he nodded. "I hear you, Lin. And while I won't deny that there will likely always be something there between Abby and me, I'm not looking to rekindle anything. Besides the fact she has a... someone, I'm not in the market. Between raising Olive and my recent divorce, I have more than enough to deal with."

Lin reached out and squeezed Clay's arm. "You're a good man, Clay. That ex-wife of yours is going to regret her decisions someday."

Clay snorted. He highly doubted it. If he was honest, he'd have to admit that Val had never liked being married. Their relationship had been all physical. Sure, they'd liked each other in the beginning, but after Olive came along and the realities of life settled in, Val had run. She thrived at parties and fundraisers, preferring to always be the center of attention. Clay, on the other hand, just wanted to provide a good life for his daughter. Even if she wanted to come back, Clay wouldn't have her. Not since he'd seen her true colors. If he ever decided to open his heart again, it would be with someone who put family first; someone who didn't run. Someone who wasn't his ex-wife or Abby.

"She will. Mark my words." Lin nodded at him, then turned and made his way back into the house.

Clay quickly unloaded the rest of Abby's boxes and then climbed into his Jeep, anxious to put distance between him and the one person he'd never been able to truly let go. But when he shoved his hand into his pocket, looking for his keys, his fingers closed around a soft piece of fabric.

Abby's lace underwear.

Son of a... He debated just taking off but couldn't stomach the thought of taking her panties home with him like some sort of creeper. That left two choices: fling them out the car window for her to find, or take them inside and discreetly hand them to her.

Damn. He pushed the car door open, jogged onto the porch, and knocked softly.

Laughter greeted him from the other side of the door, and when it opened, Faith stood there eyeing him. "Did the spiked hot cocoa change your mind?"

He shook his head. "No. I have something for Abby."

She glanced down at his empty hands and gave him a curious look. "What is it?"

His lips curved into a crooked smile. "It's top secret."

"Right." Faith rolled her eyes and pulled the door all the

way open. "She's in her bedroom. Same one as before. I'm sure you remember it."

"I think I can find it." He nodded his thanks, waved to Lin and Yvette, who were both watching him from the doorway of the kitchen, and made his way down the hall. He found Abby bent over a suitcase, her rear in the air as she rummaged around searching for something. "Need some help?"

She jerked upright and spun, pushing her blond hair out of her face. "Clay. Hi. Is there still stuff to unload out in the Jeep?"

He shook his head and stepped into her room, trying to block out all the old memories threatening to overwhelm him. It was the same room they'd spent hours in making out on her bed, where she'd told him she loved him for the first time, and where they'd planned their dreams for the future, naïve dreams that died the day she'd left for New Orleans.

She took a step back, her face flushed, and he wondered if she was remembering, too. She dropped the sweater she'd been holding on the bed and stared him in the eye as he moved closer. "Um, what is it you needed then?"

Clay smiled and closed the distance between then, enjoying her nervousness entirely too much. She might be involved with someone, but there was no mistaking that he still had an effect on her. And even if that made him a jerk, he wasn't sure he minded in that moment. Because she sure as hell still had an effect on him. He leaned in, his cheek a few inches from hers as he whispered, "You forgot something."

"Oh?"

Her body visibly swayed toward him, seemingly on its own. He knew all it would take was one small movement to have her back in his arms where she so clearly belonged. But he stood perfectly still, not touching her. *I deserve a freakin' medal*, he thought. Then he reached into his pocket, pulled out the panties, and pressed them into her hands. "As much as I appreciate you leaving them for me, I figured it would be inappropriate to keep them."

"Wha...?" She glanced down at the fabric in her hands and let out a tiny gasp as she hid them behind her back. "Where did you find these? Did my *dad* see them out there?"

He chuckled, staring down into her wide blue eyes. "No, he didn't see them. I found them peeking out from under the Jeep. I'd already snatched them up before he arrived."

"Oh, hell. Of course *you* were the one to find them. Just perfect." She closed her eyes tight and shook her head as if that could erase this moment from her memory.

"Abs?" He waited for her to open her eyes and look at him. He reached out and tucked a strand of her hair behind one ear. "Like I said earlier, they aren't anything I haven't seen before. You always did have a penchant for lace."

"Except now you have no business looking at my panties," she said, her eyes soft as she swept her gaze over him.

"I guess that's true. But I'm not sorry I did." They stared at each for a moment, the electricity sparking between them so strong it could've powered the entire town. Clay's insides were a jumble of nerves, and excitement, and pure need. Who was he kidding? Being around her was like adding air to fire. All it did was stoke the need that had never gone away.

"Clay?" she said.

"Yeah, Abs." He brushed one thumb over her cheekbone.

"I have a boyfriend... sort of. And last I heard, you have a wife. I don't think this... whatever it is, is a good idea." She swallowed and glanced away.

"Right." Clay dropped his hand and retreated to the open door. "For the record, I'm recently divorced. But point taken. Goodnight, Abigail."

She met his eyes, confusion and regret shining back at him. "Goodnight, Clay."

CHAPTER 7

"*W*hoa, is it hot in here or is it *hot* in here?" Faith fanned her face with her hand as she stood by Abby's bedroom window, watching as Clay's Jeep disappeared down the drive.

"Stop." Abby dropped her red lace panties into the top drawer of her bureau. "There's nothing there."

"Liar." Faith stared her sister down, practically daring her to deny it.

Abby pressed her lips together into a thin line. "Fine. It's obvious something's there, but it's nothing more than old history. He *just* got divorced for goodness sake."

"That's been over for well over a year, Abs. If that's your excuse, it's a poor one." Faith twisted her hair into a knot on top of her head and launched herself onto Abby's bed. "He's as available as they come."

"You're forgetting that he has a kid and I have Logan." Abby opened her closet door and carefully placed her knee-high boots next to her red leather lace-up ankle boots. It was fall on the Northern California coast, and she was ready for it.

"Logan? Seriously, Abs? I thought you said you were on a break... again."

"We are. Or were. He just told me on the phone today that he thinks that's a mistake."

"And what about you? Do you think it's a mistake? What did you say?" Faith asked.

"I don't know. Maybe? I didn't say anything. It's too much to process right this moment."

Faith tsked. "Then technically, you don't have a Logan. He broke up with you, but you don't have to take him back. Seriously, Abby, you'd pass over Clay for that guy?"

Abby straightened and turned to eye her sister. "What's wrong with Logan?"

Faith crossed her arms over her chest. "Besides being an irresponsible, spoiled, trust-fund baby?"

"Faith!" Abby frowned. "Don't be so judgmental. Besides, he's not irresponsible. He works hard."

Faith's eyes narrowed, and the disgusted look on her face was one Abby rarely saw her sister wear. "You mean you work hard and he takes credit for it."

"That's not true. He—"

"It is true. I was there, remember? I sat back and bit my tongue while you ran his gallery, ran all the promotions, and gave him a sweetheart deal on your soaps just so he could keep the lights on longer. The only reason that gallery stayed open as long as it did is because you worked your butt off while he sat in the back painting the same thing over and over again."

Abby gaped at her sister and pushed down the self-righteousness bubbling up from her gut that told her Faith was speaking everything Abby had ever thought but never voiced. Instead, she shook her head and defended him. "That artwork sold well, Faith. He was just trying to keep up with demand. It's hard to make a living running a gallery in the French Quarter."

"What are you talking about? He had an entire room full of those paintings, Abs." Her sister shook her head. "What was he doing? Building up stock for the next five years?"

"No, he didn't. That's crazy. We were always low on those paintings."

"I'm not crazy, Abby. Next time you speak to him ask him what he kept in that supply room that was always locked, the one all the way in the back. Your French Quarter witches painting was hanging on the door."

Abby opened her mouth to deny her sister's claims but promptly closed it. Why would her sister lie about such a thing? She knew Faith hadn't been the biggest fan of Logan, but she wasn't the type to make things up just to get her sister to dump someone. "You saw what was in that room?"

Her sister's cheeks flushed as she gave Abby an apologetic smile. "I might've sorta picked the lock."

"Seriously? How?"

She laughed. "I might've used my magic."

"What did you do, make an ice key?" Abby asked out of sheer curiosity. Her sister was a water witch. It always fascinated her how each of their powers differed. In Faith's case, she could manipulate water in a variety of ways. Chief among them was turning water into ice.

"Yes. But it's so dang humid down there, it was a hell of a job keeping it from melting." A look of pride flashed over her face as she mimed buffing her nails. "But I finally managed it."

"Of course you did." Abby had to admit she'd always been curious about what was in that room, but Logan had said it was just a bunch of overstock. If it was full of his paintings, she guessed that wasn't a lie. "There's one thing I don't get. Why were you so curious to see what was in that room?"

"I saw him putting some of his paintings in there one day when I came in looking for you. He was acting strange and slammed the door shut so I couldn't see what else was in there. I knew I should leave it alone, but honestly, Abs, I just didn't trust him. I knew he was your boyfriend, and I might've been totally off, but I was just trying to protect you. I'm sorry. I know sneaking around was wrong, but I don't regret it. Now I know he isn't the one for you."

Logan's voice sounded in her head. *I love you, Abs.* Had that just been a few hours ago? And did he really mean it? How could he love her if he'd been lying to her for months? "Why didn't you say anything before?"

Faith shrugged. "I tried, but he was always around. By the time I got home and learned the gallery was closing, I just felt bad for the guy. I don't know. I guess I should've tried harder, but what did it really matter by then? You two were on a break, and the gallery was already lost, so you didn't have to deal with it anymore."

If he'd lied to her about his paintings, what else had he lied to her about? Or had his ego just been too fragile to admit people didn't want to spend hundreds of dollars on his art? Her stomach started to ache, and she pressed her palm against her abdomen, suddenly wishing for some of her mother's calming potion.

"You okay?" Faith asked her.

"Yeah. Just stunned. And betrayed."

"Oh, no, Abby. I'm so sorry." Faith jumped off the bed and wrapped her arm around Abby's shoulders. "I never should have snuck around like that. The last thing I'd want to do is shatter any trust—"

"Faith," Abby cut her off. "Not betrayed by you. By Logan. He lied to me... for months. Thanks for telling me. I guess I have some thinking to do."

"I'm sorry I didn't say anything sooner. I should have. You deserved to know."

"Don't worry about it." She pasted a smile on. "I guess it's time for me to make that break permanent."

Faith gave her a hug, and when she pulled back she gave Abby a sly smile. "After you do that, don't forget there is a hot dad in town who's dying to see you in those red panties."

Abby's eyes widened. "Were you spying on us?"

"Not on purpose." Faith laughed. "But I might've caught the tail end of that conversation."

Abby swatted her sister. "You're a creeper."

"I have to get my thrills somewhere." Faith grinned, hooked her arm through her sister's, and tugged her toward the door. "Come on. Yvette's got dinner in the oven."

"IF WE GET THE CROP TREATED BY THE MORNING, I THINK they'll be fine," Lincoln Townsend said, glancing over his shoulder as he stepped through the back door. Something had been bothering him all through dinner, and before Yvette could set out dessert, he'd asked Isaac to take one more look at the south side of the orchard. They'd only been gone twenty minutes, but judging by her father's comments, he'd come to some sort of conclusion.

Isaac kicked off his muddy boots and followed his father-in-law into the kitchen. "Just as long as we don't wait any longer. We don't want to risk losing the entire crop."

"Something wrong out in the orchard?" Abigail asked from her spot at the bar.

Isaac glanced her way and nodded. "Fungus." The tall man turned to her father. "Are you going to give Clay a call, or do you want me to do it? If we catch him early enough, he might be able to get it done so it's ready first thing in the morning."

"Clay?" Abby blurted, her body still heated from their earlier exchange. "You want to call him? Why?"

Her father gave her a sympathetic pat on the arm. "Half the orchard has developed a fungus, and if we don't treat the trees right away, it could spell trouble for the crop. Clay is our resident earth witch. It's too bad we didn't know what was going on when he was here earlier."

"And you want him to make the potion?" she asked, already knowing the answer. Of course they did. Hadn't her father already said he was the resident earth witch? "What happened to Tally? Did she retire or something?"

"Yep. About six months ago," her dad confirmed.

"And she moved to Scottsdale with her new husband," Isaac said with a snicker.

Abby raised her eyebrows in question. "That's funny why?"

"He's nineteen years younger than her and doesn't have a magical bone in his body. It's pretty obvious why she went for him. Yvette caught them making out in the stacks at the book store. He had his hand down—"

"That's enough," Lin said mildly.

Abby laughed. "Good for her."

"You don't think that's just a little scandalous?" Isaac asked, not bothering to hide his judgment.

"Maybe. But who cares? If they're both happy, then more power to them."

Isaac let out a small snort of disapproval. "It's just not right if you ask me."

"I didn't," Abby said sweetly, refraining from rolling her eyes at him. *What a jerk*, she thought and changed the subject. "Don't you have a call to make?"

"Right. Let's hope Clay doesn't have plans tonight."

The idea of Clay on a date with another woman made Abby's stomach turn, and she suddenly felt like she was twenty again, suffering from a broken heart when she learned Clay had run off and married an aspiring actress.

"Or you could give him a break and get Abby to make the treatment," Noel said, appearing out of nowhere. She hadn't said more than a handful of words at dinner, and none of them had been directed at Abby. "It's not like it'd take her long."

"You know I can't do that, Noel," Abby said automatically.

"You mean won't," her sister accused. "Yet, you infuse your magic into your lotions and special soaps and peddle them to unsuspecting tourists every single day. Hypocrite much?"

"Noel," her father said, his tone suddenly tired. "Leave your sister alone."

Noel glared at Abby then turned on her heel and left the room.

Abigail worried the hem of her sweater, once again consumed by guilt and anxiety. "I'm sorry, Dad. I know the treatment potion isn't a big deal, I just…" She let her voice trail off, not knowing how to explain her inability to use her magic for anything other than her soaps and lotions.

"There's nothing to apologize for," her father said, wrapping his arm around her shoulder and pulling her in for a sideways hug. "Your sister just doesn't understand. She'll come around… eventually."

Abby nodded, grateful for her father's comfort, but she knew his words were hollow. Noel would never understand. It had been a decade since she'd cast her last spell in Keating Hollow. If Noel hadn't come around by now, she wasn't going to.

"I'll talk to her," Faith said, already following Noel into the next room.

"Faith—" Abby started, but her sister waved her off.

"Someone has to talk some sense into her," Faith called over her shoulder as she disappeared down the hall.

Abby met Yvette's gaze across the kitchen. Yvette shook her head indicating Faith's mission was a lost cause. Abby sighed, slipped off the stool, and headed into the living room to spend some time with her niece.

~

Abby lay in her bed staring at the ceiling, her body bone-tired, but unable to sleep. Between seeing Clay and hearing her sister's revelations about Logan, her mind was racing. She'd only been home less than twenty-four hours, and her life was already in a tail-spin. The pull to Clay was undeniable and always had been for as long as she could remember. She just hadn't realized that even after ten years that attraction hadn't faded… not even one little bit. And it was unsettling.

No matter the issues between her and Logan, she was still in some sort of relationship with him. Was a break an official breakup? She wasn't sure, especially after the last conversation she'd had with him. But she owed it to him and herself to figure out what she wanted and fast, especially if she was starting to daydream about another man.

Agitated, she kicked the covers off, wrapped herself in her flannel robe, and headed down the hall toward the kitchen. A soft light spilled from the kitchen into the hall, and when Abby rounded the corner, her lips curved into a small smile as she spotted her father sitting at the bar, two mugs in front of him.

"I thought I might be seeing you tonight." He nudged one of the mugs, indicating it was for her.

Abby took a seat next to him and noted he was wrapped in his own flannel robe and had pulled on mismatched socks. She giggled. "Still color-blind I see."

He glanced down at his robe. "What? It's plaid. How can I go wrong with this?"

She pointed at his feet. "It's your socks. One is purple tones and the other is greens."

He glanced down and smirked. "I knew that. I was just testing you."

"Sure." Abby lifted the mug to her lips and took a sip. "How'd you know?"

"Know what?" he asked. "About the fungus?"

"No, that I wouldn't be able to sleep."

Her dad reached out and placed his hand over hers. "A dad just knows."

"More like an earth witch can tell when another earth witch is a little unsettled," Abby said, cutting right to the chase.

He chuckled. "That, too. I could always read you better than I could your sisters."

"Much to my dismay," Abby said with a teasing tone in her voice. "You never let me get away with anything."

Her dad took a long sip of his coffee and nodded in agreement. "Kept you out of trouble a time or two as well, if I recall."

"More like kept me locked in my room while Yvette and Noel were out witchin' it up."

"Poor, Abby. But then I seem to remember you were the one who never got herself grounded and had more free rein when you weren't trying to pull one over on your old pops, so I'm thinking you didn't suffer too much."

"You got me there." She squeezed her dad's fingers, love bubbling over for the man who'd raised her. Emotion welled up and she forced it back down, unwilling to let herself even think about his cancer diagnosis. She was here to spend time with him, to be here when he needed her, not breakdown and lean on him for support.

"It's going to be okay, Abby-girl," he said softly.

"Of course it is." Her tone was too bright, too cheerful, and she was certain he saw right through her.

"Tell me about what's been bothering you tonight. I know it isn't your old dad. Feels more like matters of the heart."

She stared at the mug in front of her. "It's eerie how you do that, you know."

"Want to talk about it? Is it because Clay's back home?"

Abby let out a sigh. "Yes. No. I don't know."

"He still cares for you."

She glanced at her father, her mouth hanging open. "Did he tell you that?"

Lin chuckled. "No, my girl. He'd probably bite his tongue off before he confessed his feelings to me. But he sure didn't come over here tonight to drop off beer samples. That, my darling, was certainly so he could see you."

She'd suspected that might be the case. Why else would he volunteer to haul all her crap over? He knew her family would help without any fuss. It was the Townsend way. Warmth spread through her just knowing Clay was still taking care of her even after she'd left him all those years ago.

Lin turned to her, his eyes searching hers. "Or is it Logan? Are you unsettled because you're away from him?"

Abby let out a surprised snort then clasped her hand over her mouth, mortified at her reaction. He'd been her significant other for the majority of the past two years, and she'd acted as if he didn't even matter. "Um, I didn't mean to do that."

"Yes you did." Lin's eyes twinkled with amusement. "It's okay you know. You don't have to act like he's the love of your life. Especially since he isn't."

"How do you know? You haven't even met him." Her father had come to New Orleans a couple of times to visit her, but not since she'd started dating Logan.

"You forget we share a unique connection." He gave her that

knowing smile again. "But even if we didn't, any idiot could figure out he isn't the one. Will you do something for me?"

"What's that?" she asked.

"Give yourself a break. You don't owe anyone anything. Not Logan. Not Clay. Not your sisters. Not even me."

"Dad, that's not—"

He held up his hand. "Family is family, and I love you for being here. But the truth is you're here for yourself as much as you are for me. I meant what I said. You don't owe any of us anything. And that man you've been dating back in New Orleans? He's lucky you stood by him while he tried his hand at being an artist. Not the other way around."

Abby blinked. "You've been talking to Faith."

"A little. And I know I haven't met the man, but from what I heard, he doesn't deserve my talented and beautiful daughter." He wrapped his arm around her shoulders and pulled her in close.

The unease in her chest dissipated, and she smiled to herself. "You say that about everyone who dates your daughters."

He didn't respond, but instead just held onto her, letting her soak up his love. Finally, he said, "I love you, Abby-girl. Be true to yourself."

"I love you, too, Dad." She glanced up at him, meeting his gaze. "And thanks. This was exactly what I needed."

He kissed the top of her head. "Now get to bed. This old man needs his beauty sleep."

"You don't look a day over forty," she said with a wink.

"That's good to hear. I'll be sure to tell Clair she's landed herself a catch." Clair was the woman he'd been dating for the last fifteen years. Abby had always assumed they'd get married someday, but the pair of them had remained content with their Friday night dinners and Sunday morning brunch. Abby was glad her father had someone, but she was also sad he'd given up on marriage after her mother had broken his heart twenty years ago.

"I'm sure she already knows." Abby kissed her father's cheek and shuffled back toward her room.

"Abby?"

She paused and glanced back over her shoulder. "Yeah, Dad?"

"What you said about me thinking no one deserves my daughters..."

"What about it?"

"There's one who does."

Abby waited for him to continue, but he just smiled as he got out of his chair and headed toward his room on the other end of the house.

"You're not just gonna leave it at that, are you?" she called after him.

He waved without looking back, and she heard him laughing to himself as his bedroom door closed with a soft click.

68

CHAPTER 8

*T*he fog rolled over the coastal mountains and settled over the Keating Hollow valley. Clay stood on the front porch of the brewery, breathing deep, letting the air and the smell of redwoods settle him. He hadn't slept well the night before.

First, he couldn't get Abby or her red lace off his mind. Then just when he'd finally begun to drift off, an overwhelming sense of dread had hit him. At three a.m. he sat bolt upright in bed, wide awake with the deep-seated need to check on Olive. Only she wasn't down the hall in her bed. She was over seven hundred miles away with her mother and god knew who else.

He wasn't one to ignore instinct and had immediately called his daughter's cell phone. She'd answered on the forth ring, her voice groggy and full of sleep. After assuring him she was fine, he'd gently told her to go back to sleep and that he'd talk to her in the morning.

Of course, that had resulted in a seven a.m. call from Val,

who'd taken the opportunity to call him every depraved thing under the sun. All because he'd been worried. How had he ever gotten involved with someone so toxic?

He knew the answer to that but was unwilling to dwell on it. After Abby had left, he'd needed someone, anyone, to help him through the pain of losing her. And Val had been there. Too bad it took him far too long to figure out she was the polar opposite of what he was really looking for.

"Morning boss," Rhys, his assistant, said as he made his way toward the front door. "Taking a moment before all hell breaks loose?"

"Huh?"

Rhys's brow pinched as he frowned. "The Main Street festival. We're hosting a tasting, remember?"

"Right." Clay shook his head. He'd completely forgotten. After his infuriating calls with Val and seeing Abby again, it was amazing he'd managed to even remember to come into work at all. "We better get to it then."

Rhys nodded and a moment later, Clay followed him into the pub.

~

"WE NEED ANOTHER KEG OF CARAMEL FEST, AND BELIEVE IT OR not, we're completely out of Pumpkin Spice," Clay told Rhys as he poured yet another glass of Chocolate Stout from the tap.

"Geez. Those witches are really into their pumpkin, aren't they?" Rhys asked, grabbing a couple bottles of Moon Pale Ale.

Clay laughed. "Why do you think I insisted on producing it? I swear we can add pumpkin spice to just about anything in October and make a killing."

"Just don't put it on my sweet potato fries," Yvette said with a shudder from her spot at the end of the bar. "Enough is enough."

"That's a special order," Clay confirmed. "No fries will be adulterated on my watch unless requested."

"Good." Yvette took a long sip of her Chocolate Stout then dug into her burger, ignoring the flurry of activity going on behind her.

Half the town must be here, Clay thought as he watched the crowd wait patiently for samples of his new beer. And so far, all the flavors had been a hit. He'd been a little nervous when they'd rolled out the fall lineup. Lincoln Townsend brewed a damn fine beer, but he'd been a traditionalist, preferring instead to put out classic pale ales, lagers, porters, and wheat beers. Before Clay had been made master brewer, the closest any of the Keating Hollow brews had come to a flavor was their porter, which naturally had a faint chocolate taste. At least one aspect of his life was going well.

He used a handkerchief to wipe his brow and then filled another tray of samples.

"You didn't wait for me," a familiar feminine voice said.

Clay jerked his head up and spotted Abby claiming the seat right next to Yvette. The two sisters were total opposites, one dark and one light. But the way they sat, both of their postures exactly the same, their heads tilted at the same angle, there was no mistaking they were from the same bloodline.

"I ordered your lunch, though," Yvette said and signaled to Sadie, the brewery's part time waitress. "She's here."

Sadie nodded and disappeared into the kitchen. A few moments later, she emerged with chowder in a bread bowl and a house salad. She glanced over at Clay. "I need a Chocolate Stout, please."

"You got it."

Abby stiffened slightly but didn't turn to acknowledge him, and he nearly laughed. She was all too aware he was there and was doing everything in her power to ignore him. Well, he'd see about that. He shuffled down the bar and stood right in front of the two sisters.

"Good afternoon, ladies." He grinned at them. "Sluffing off again?"

Yvette rolled her eyes. "Sluffing off, my pink patootie. I was at work, but someone is giving out free beer, and apparently the people of this town would rather drink beer than shop for books. So I gave in and decided to meet my sister for a late lunch. As it is, I'm not even sure we're going to bring in enough today to cover Brinn's paycheck."

Clay vaguely recalled the woman who Yvette had hired a few months ago. She was a new witch in town; a cousin of Wanda's, if he remembered correctly. Another air witch, he thought, making her a perfect fit to stock books. They were skilled at moving things through the air. "I'm sure people's pocketbooks will open up once they've downed enough hops."

Abby laughed. "That always worked at the Art Market in New Orleans."

Clay placed his elbow on the bar and leaned in close to her, unable to resist the ever-present pull. "And what about you, Abby? What are your plans while you're in town? Beach? Hiking? Reckless golf cart rides with Wanda?"

"Actually, Clay, if you must know, while all of those things sound like a wonderful vacation, I'll actually be working most of the time. I have orders to fill for the holiday season."

"She's taking over the brew shed," Yvette said, her lips curving into an amused smile.

"You are?" Clay jerked back, nearly knocking over Sadie in the process.

"Watch it," the petite blonde said, steadying him with both hands. "People are working back here."

"Sorry," Clay muttered and turned his attention back to Abby. "You're going to be working here? For how long? A week? Two?"

Abby tilted her head to the side, studying him. "Why? Does it bother you that I'll be here?"

"No!" he said too quickly, his voice entirely too high. Zeus and Hades, he was being an idiot. He cleared his throat and tried again. "I mean, of course not. I was just wondering how long the brew shed would be occupied."

"Why? No one uses it," Yvette said, her eyes narrowed in suspicion.

Clay knew what she was thinking. She thought he was trying to figure out how long Abby would be working less than ten feet from him. But it wasn't that... or at least not entirely that. He actually used the brew shed when he was working on new recipes. It had been Lin's original brewing building back when they'd first started the pub over forty years ago. Today, there was state of the art equipment in the main building, which rendered the shed obsolete. But it had running water, heat, a stove, and it was quiet, which was what he needed when he was working on a new recipe.

"I figure I'll be here through the holidays," Abby said. "And I'll need to work while I'm here. So if my using the shed is a problem for you, I need to know sooner rather than later so I can make other arrangements."

"No." Clay shook his head, trying not to notice the thread of anticipation winding its way through him. Knowing he'd see her most days for the next three months stripped away the stress of the last year that had been wearing him down, and he felt like a damned teenager again, eager to just be near the pretty girl he couldn't stop thinking about. "It's not a problem at all."

Her eyes sparkled under the lights as she smiled up at him. "Good."

"Oh, hells bells," Yvette said, rolling her eyes. "I'm out of here before the two of you burst into flames from all the sparks flying around." She climbed off her stool, tossed a couple bills on the counter, and strode out of the pub.

Abby eyed the bills on the counter. "Are we paying for our meals now?"

Clay shook his head. "No. All the Townsends eat free here. That's Sadie's tip."

"Right. Of course." Abby rummaged around in her bag and matched the bills her sister had left. Then she raised her beer in a salute. "To working together for the next few months."

Clay popped the cap on a bottle of porter, clinked it to her mug, and echoed, "To working together."

They held each other's gazes as they each took a long sip. For Clay, it was as if the pub, his fellow employees, and all the customers faded away and all that was left was Abby—until he heard a cry and the clatter of glass shattering on the tile floor.

He jerked upright, his gaze scanning the front of house. Then he spotted Sadie sprawled on the floor amidst spilled beer and a pile of glass shards. Blood stained her left arm and soaked into her white Keating Hollow Brewery T-shirt.

"Sadie!" Abby jumped up off her stool and ran to the woman's side. After taking one look at her, she called, "Clay, get the first aid kit and some clean towels."

He grabbed a stack of clean towels and tossed them to her. Then he rushed to the back room, retrieving the first aid kit. When he joined Abby at Sadie's side, Abby had Sadie's arm bandaged with a couple of towels. Blood had already seeped through both layers.

SOUL OF THE WITCH

"Forget the kit. She needs a healer. Fast," Abby said.

Clay didn't hesitate. He just scooped Sadie up into his arms and started moving toward the front doors. Just before he walked through the threshold he called over his shoulder, "Abby, keep an eye on things until I get back."

"You got it," he heard her respond. Then he started to run.

CHAPTER 9

The sun had long since set when Abby finally locked the front doors of Keating Hollow Brewery. She hadn't seen or heard from Clay since he'd taken Sadie to the healer, and she was more than a little worried. The only upside was that the pub had been so busy, she hadn't had time to stress about them much.

She couldn't remember a time when she'd seen the pub so successful. Practically everyone who'd come in had proclaimed themselves regulars, and it appeared Clay's brews were a huge hit with the town. But the thing that had put a smile on her face was that while they all expressed how much they missed seeing her father every day, they'd also made it clear they approved of the work Clay was doing.

For some reason, their praise filled her with a sense of pride as if Clay was still hers.

"Let it go, Abs," she told herself and got to work sweeping up the floors. By the time she had the tiles mopped and gleaming, every muscle in her body was aching to relax. But she still hadn't unloaded her dad's truck, the entire reason she'd come to the pub in the first place.

"Looks good, Abby," Rhys said from his spot behind the bar. Much to her relief, he'd volunteered to stay and make sure the kitchen was in order. The bar was spotless, the kegs restocked, and the cash register balanced. "Ready?"

"You go ahead," she said, waving him off. "I still have a couple things to do."

His eyebrows shot up. "Like what? I don't think I've seen this place so clean since Yvette took over for a week while your dad went to visit you in New Orleans."

Abby laughed. That was no surprise. Yvette was the type of person who couldn't go to bed unless her kitchen was spotless and any clutter had been put away. "I just need to unload some stuff from Dad's truck."

"Need help?" he asked, already moving toward her.

"No, no. You've been here for hours. Go home. I've got this." She gave him an encouraging smile and moved to unlock the door for him. "Rest up. I know you come in early."

The yawn he couldn't quite suppress proved her point.

"See there? You're exhausted. Go on. Get out of here," she ordered.

"I'm not going to wait for you to tell me a third time." He gave her a grateful smile and disappeared into the night.

Abby walked over to the bar, filled a glass with stout from the tap, and slumped onto one of the stools, her entire body sagging with relief. Damn, when had she gotten so out of shape? Back when she'd been in high school, she'd spent many evenings waitressing and couldn't remember ever feeling quite as exhausted as she did in the moment.

She sat back into the stool and jerked when her butt started to vibrate. Hopeful it was Clay calling, she grabbed her phone, and her heart sank when she saw it was Logan. She grimaced.

That wasn't the reaction she was supposed to have when her sort-of significant other called.

After mentally scolding herself, she accepted the call and said in a bright tone, "Hey, what's up?"

"Check your email," he said, his tone carrying an air of excitement.

"What?" Abby frowned. "Why?"

"You'll never believe what happened today. It's crazy."

"Okay, what happened today?" she asked, stifling a yawn. Her eyes watered, and she wanted nothing more than to climb into her bed back at her dad's and sleep for a good solid twelve hours.

"Guess. Go on. You'll never guess."

"Um, I don't know. You sold some of your paintings?" There was silence on the other end of the line, and for a moment she thought the call was dropped. "Logan? You still there?"

She heard him let out an exaggerated sigh. "Yes, I'm here. It doesn't have anything to do with my paintings."

"Oh." Frustration rose up in the back of her throat, and she wanted to scream just to let it out. She knew that tone. He wasn't just irritated; he was pissed she'd brought up his paintings. Well, dammit, he was the one who'd told her to guess. How was she supposed to know what his big news was? For the first year and a half of their relationship, everything had revolved around art... or more specifically, *his* art. Was it any wonder she'd guess he'd had some success? "Um, you had a deal go through?"

"That's better, but that's not why I called."

All of his excitement had vanished, and it was clear to Abby that he blamed her for taking the wind out of his sails. Well, that was just too damned bad. She wasn't a mind reader, and it wasn't like she'd said anything out of line. "I give," she said, forcing some levity into her tone. "What's the big news?"

"It was supposed to be a surprise."

"It still is," she said with a laugh, "since I clearly have no idea what you're trying to tell me."

"That's obvious."

"What?" She pulled the phone away from her ear and stared at it in disbelief. When she pressed it to her ear again, she said, "Are you seriously angry at me right now because I can't read your mind?"

"No, Abigail, I'm frustrated because it seems you haven't been listening to me for the last six months. It would be nice if you could just support my choices instead of always bringing up my failed art gallery."

Shock rippled through her, and she suddenly remembered what Faith had said about him hiding dozens of his paintings from her. "I'm sorry," she said automatically, even though she hadn't said one word about the gallery. That hardly mattered when it was obvious he was harboring a seriously bruised ego. "I won't bring it or your art up again."

"Thank you."

Silence hung between them, but this time Abby was determined to wait him out. She still didn't feel like she'd done anything wrong. And if he wanted to tell her his news, she wasn't going to waste any more energy on prying it out of him. Honestly, after her drive across the country and her long day working at the brewery, she just didn't have it in her to work her way through Logan's issues.

"You know what, Abby? I have a meeting to get to. Just check your email and call and let me know what you think."

"Okay," she said, but silence greeted her response, and when she pulled the phone away she noted the call had ended. Shaking her head, she glared at the phone and said, "Asshat."

"Trouble in paradise?" a deep voice said softly from behind her.

Clay.

He was back. The tension drained from her shoulders, and when she turned around and looked into his concerned dark eyes, peace settled in her soul. All of the angst she felt from talking to Logan disappeared, and she felt *right* in a way she hadn't in a very long time. She didn't want to explore what it meant, but in that moment she was just glad she was in the presence of someone she wanted desperately to be her friend again.

"It would appear so," she confirmed and gave him a weak smile. "Seems I'm not winning any girlfriend-of-the-year awards." Why had she said girlfriend? She wasn't even sure what she was anymore. Damn, she really needed to settle things with Logan and the sooner the better, for her own peace of mind.

"If you aren't, I'm certain your asshat has no idea just how lucky he is."

Her smile widened. "That's sweet of you to say. Thanks."

He shrugged. "It's just the truth."

"You don't know that. As far as you know, I could be the biggest witch on the planet these days. What if I stole all the money out of his wallet before I left town?"

"Did you?"

"No."

"Of course you didn't. I bet you filled his refrigerator with his favorite pie and left him your famous lasagna in his freezer."

She laughed, and her insides warmed with the knowledge he still knew her so well. "Close. Homemade caramel ice cream and étouffée."

"See, you're still the same sweet girl you were years ago, and if he doesn't see it, that's his problem."

They held each other's gazes for a beat or two then Abby whispered, "Thanks."

"You're welcome."

Abby gave him a grateful smile then frowned as she remembered the reason she was working in the pub in the first place. "How's Sadie?"

"She's doing better now that she's stitched up. It'll be a few weeks before she can work, but she'll be fine."

"Oh, good." Abby let out a sigh of relief. That gash had been ugly.

Clay walked over to her and offered her a hand to help her down off the stool. "Now, why are you still here?"

After she gained her footing, she dropped his hand and stuffed her hands into her pockets. "I still need to unload my dad's truck. We were so busy here I never got around to it."

"Well then, let's unload it." He started walking toward the front door, but Abby didn't move.

"You don't have to do that. You already moved it all from my car to my dad's garage."

"Abby, you just spent all day doing my job. I think I can help you unload a few boxes." He unlocked the door and jerked his head, indicating she should follow. "Come on. You look exhausted. Let's get this done so you can get some rest."

Her feet seemed to move all on their own, and when she caught up with him, she touched his arm and said, "Thanks."

His hand pressed against the small of her back and in a low, gruff voice, he said, "Anything for you, Abs."

CHAPTER 10

*A*bby walked into her dad's house with a warm glow in her chest. She couldn't remember the last time she'd felt so... light. Clay was exactly the sort of friend she needed right then—fun, supportive, and easy going. It was amazing that they could still slip into their comfortable friendship even after all the history they shared.

The house was dark except for a light over the stove. Humming, Abby made herself some hot cocoa then sat down at the bar and opened her laptop. After printing out a list of her recent orders, she opened her email.

Her good mood immediately fled when she saw the unopened email from Logan. A sigh escaped her lips just as she heard a thump, followed by a moan, come from somewhere in the vicinity of her dad's bedroom.

"Dad?" She hoped off the stool and hurried to her father's door. Knocking, she said, "Hey, Dad, you okay?"

Fear rushed over her, and she knocked again.

The soft shuffle of footsteps sounded right before he pulled the door open and gave her a weak smile. "I'm fine, Abby. Just tripped over the ottoman."

Abby blinked, then scanned his slightly hunched body and noted his hand resting on his abdomen. "You don't look fine, Dad."

He closed his eyes and shook his head slightly. "Just worn out and suffering a little nausea after today's treatment."

"You had a treatment today?" she asked, her mouth hanging open in shock. "How come you didn't tell me? Why didn't Yvette say anything? I had lunch with her. Geez, Dad, who took you?"

He grimaced and visibly swallowed. "No one. I took myself."

"Why?" Abby was genuinely confused. "You didn't need to do that. If I'd known, I would've been here. It's part of the reason I came home in the first place."

"Abby," he said, his voice raspy with exhaustion. "I'm a grown man. I can get myself to the hospital and back for treatment." He sucked in a breath and turned his head away as his coloring turned a sickly green. "I—" Her father turned and rushed to his bathroom. Within seconds, she heard the retching.

"Oh, Dad," she said under her breath and retreated to the kitchen where she rustled up some saltine crackers and a glass of ginger ale. She paused to glance at her studio out back. Guilt ate away at her conscience. There was a time when she'd have whipped up a potion to eliminate those nausea symptoms. But that was a long time ago, and she was out of practice. If she'd known her dad was going to start treatment already, she would've found a healer and stocked the house with some anti-nausea potion.

She hurried back to his room, placed the crackers and ginger ale on his nightstand, and paced while she waited for him to return. When he finally emerged from the bathroom, she did her best to hide her worry and rushed to help him back to the bed.

This time he slipped his arm over her shoulder and leaned on her for support. "That chemo really takes it out of you."

"Here. Get back in bed. I brought crackers."

"Thanks, Abs," he said and let out a relieved sigh as he sat back down on the bed. He bypassed the crackers and took a sip of the ginger ale. After making a face, he put the beverage back down on the nightstand and picked up the television remote. "Want to watch a movie?"

"Sure, Dad. If you want."

He clicked the television on and surfed until he found a John Wayne movie. Grinning at her, he patted the other side of the bed. "Get comfy. There's a marathon running."

Abby groaned but chuckled good naturedly "Seriously? The Duke, again? Maybe you should try something from this decade."

Her dad propped himself up on two pillows and shook his head. "You can't beat perfection, Abby."

She just shook her head and sat leaning against his headboard. Five minutes later, her dad was out of bed again for round two in the bathroom. The sounds of his vomiting brought tears to her eyes.

Why him? She asked the universe for the hundredth time since her sister had called to give her the news of his diagnosis. He didn't deserve this. No one did, but Lincoln Townsend especially. Her father was the rock of the Townsend family, the steady hand who'd always been there for each of them, through heartbreaks and failed tests and other disappointments with no mother to rely on. Lin had been left to raise four girls on his own and had done it with a whole lot of love and grace, never once complaining about his lot in life. There wasn't a day that went by that she didn't feel loved and cherished by her father.

The sound of water running pulled Abby out of her thoughts and she hastily wiped at her damp eyes. She didn't want her father to see her upset. He'd only worry about her, and she didn't want to add herself to his list of things to worry about. She was there to support him this time, not the other way around.

When he finally emerged, his face had turned ashen, and there were dark circles under his eyes. He'd also changed out of his jeans and into flannel pajama bottoms and a fresh T-shirt. She pushed herself off the bed and hurried to give him a helping hand, but he waved her off.

"I'm all right. Just need to lie down and get some sleep," he said.

"Sure. Let me just—"

"I *said* I'm all right."

Abby backed off, understanding he hated appearing weak. She knew this was his way of proving to himself that he could get through this, just like when he'd taken himself to the doctor and neglected to tell any of them. She waited while he sat on his bed and took another sip of the ginger ale. When the liquid hit his lips, he grimaced again.

"I can get you something else. Water? I can call the pharmacy and see if they have anything for the nausea."

"I've already got some pills, Abby," he said softly. "I took some right after the treatment. They said even with the pills, vomiting wasn't unusual."

Abby scoffed. "Then what's the point?"

His tired eyes met hers. "Without them, I think I'd be curled up on the bathroom floor all night instead of here in front of the television."

"I see." Abby crossed her arms over her chest and frowned.

She was grateful he had something that was partially helping, but was that the best they could do?

Her dad climbed under the covers, and without even turning the television off, he rolled over on his side and closed his eyes.

Abby let out a long breath, left the remote on his nightstand, and turned off the light as she said, "Night, Dad. I'll be here if you need anything."

He pulled the covers up higher on his shoulder and said, "I know you are. G'night."

Abby closed the door behind her and finally let go of the tears she'd been holding back for the last hour. A tiny sob escaped her throat as she sat on the leather couch and buried her face in her hands as all her fear rushed to the surface.

It was as if his cancer diagnosis had finally become real. Seeing him sick, knowing it was from the chemotherapy, it had been a gut punch. She knew he was up for fighting this battle, believed he'd kick cancer's butt and come out the other side of this stronger than ever. But that didn't change the fact that the little girl inside of her had just watched her hero be taken down a few notches by the one villain she couldn't fight for him.

Her dad was no longer infallible, and it hurt too much being forced to confront that reality.

Abby got up, moved to the kitchen, and grabbed a fistful of tissues to clean up her face. After she dried her tears, she sat back down at her computer and once again took a peek at her email.

"Oh, hell," she muttered, spotting the email from Logan. She was in no mood to deal with whatever it was he wanted to surprise her with and was going to log out, but the email preview caught her attention: *The Witch's Ball.*

She clicked the message. It read: *In our meeting today, I met*

*the mayor. He was impressed with our vision for revitalizing the
defunct amusement part, and he insisted we join him at the New
Orleans Witch's Ball. I know how much you wanted to go last year.
The tickets were damned expensive, but you're worth it, babe. You
can thank me by wearing something sexy. Can't wait to see you in a
few days. We'll make a long weekend of it. I already booked you a
flight.*

*P.S. Don't forget to pick me up something to wear. I have
meetings nonstop until you get here. You still have my measurements,
right?*

There was an attachment with an airline ticket in her name.
The flight from San Francisco was in two days, leaving at
six-thirty a.m.

Abby sat on the stool, staring at the email. This was a joke,
right? Was he that obtuse that he'd buy her a ticket and expect
her to go back to New Orleans just a few days after she'd
arrived home? After she'd already told him that leaving after
only being in town for two *weeks* didn't feel right? Was he
insane? The longer she stared at the email, the angrier she
became. Her emotions were already frayed after watching her
dad deal with the aftermath of his chemotherapy. She didn't
have it in her to care one whit for Logan's fragile ego.

Selfish son of a witch. Those tickets weren't for her. They
were for him, to help him cozy up to the city officials in hopes
of getting their support. No doubt he'd have some meeting set
up he'd make her go to. Even if he didn't, his blatant disregard
for her need to be near her dad right then was enough to make
her want to scream.

She hit Reply and started typing.

*You're a piece of work. I hope you sprang for a refundable airline
ticket, because I'm not going anywhere.*

P.S. Get your own damned clothes. I'm not your personal

assistant. I'm not even your girlfriend. Not anymore. Find someone else to manipulate. I'm done.

Before she could stop to think about it, she hit Send and slammed the laptop closed. Breathing heavily, she got up and started to pace. Her heart hammered against her ribcage. Had she really just ended whatever it was they had in an email? She nodded. Yes, yes she had. She deserved better. Much, much better.

Her time with Clay that evening had been illuminating. Not because she was all too aware that she still felt something for him, but because he was so thoughtful. That was the second time in two days he'd gone out of his way to help her and asked for nothing in return. And the thing was he'd always been that way. He'd never acted as if his goals, his job, or his needs were more important than hers. Her short time with him earlier in the evening reminded her of what it felt like to be with someone who truly cared for someone other than himself.

Whatever did or didn't happen between her and Clay in the future didn't matter. He'd shown her something she'd forgotten, and she was grateful.

Her phone buzzed. Abby scowled when she saw Logan's face flash on the screen, and she declined the call. The phone buzzed again.

She gritted her teeth, knowing he'd keep trying until she picked up. *Well, let him,* she thought and ignored it while she made another cup of cocoa. True to form Logan continued to relentlessly blow up her phone. Finally, she sucked in a fortifying breath and answered. "What do you want, Logan?"

"What the hell, Abigail? I bought you an amazing gift and then you break up with me in an email? Is this how you repay me?"

"Repay you?" Abby spat out. "For what? Ignoring me when I said I needed to be here for my dad?"

"Oh, come on. Your sisters are there. You can come home for three days."

Abby's face heated, and the desire to scream nearly made her head explode. She might have, too, if her father hadn't been in the other room trying to sleep. She counted to five in her head then said, "I'm already home, Logan. I'm not coming back to New Orleans. You'll just have to figure out how to move forward without me."

"What do you mean you're not coming back to New Orleans? Of course you are. What about my meeting in two weeks?"

She closed her eyes and wondered if she was speaking an entirely different language. Had he always been so self-absorbed and selfish or had his personality shifted over the last months? She couldn't imagine herself being attracted to someone so dismissive who ignored practically everything she said. "Logan, listen carefully. I am not coming back to New Orleans anytime soon. The earliest would be after the new year, if at all. Right now, I'm here with my dad and my sisters where I belong. And no, I can't just leave and let my sisters deal with things. I'm here for me as much as I am for them and my dad. So... just stop."

Dead silence.

After a moment Abby said, "Goodbye, Logan."

"Abby," he said, drawing out her name. "Come on, baby. Don't be mad. I made a mistake. I'm sorry. I'll call you tomorrow and we can work this out."

"No!" she barked into the phone. "Do not call me. I'm not just mad, Logan. I'm done."

"But—"

"Goodbye." She ended the call, and when he called right back again, she declined and blocked his number.

A strange mix of relief and regret washed over her when

SOUL OF THE WITCH

the phone was finally silent. It was done. She was officially free. And while a weight eased off her chest, she couldn't help the fresh wave of tears that stung her eyes. Abby blinked furiously, refusing to cry over Logan. Leaving New Orleans had shown her just how much he'd been using her. Breaking it off was the right thing to do, and she'd be better off for it, but she couldn't help feeling a little bit like a failure. She'd tried hard to make that relationship work. Too hard, probably. Now she just needed to let it go. It was time.

CHAPTER 11

*A*bby stood at the entrance of the farmers market, a smile tugging at her lips. She'd spent the last three days keeping an eye on her dad and helping him with the orchard. The only time she'd ventured off the property was to mail out the few orders that had come in. Now her stock was depleted, and she had to get serious about rebuilding her inventory, but not before she took advantage of the gorgeous autumn day and picked up a few treasures.

The market was filled with artists and small-crop farmers, and she couldn't wait to visit every booth to get to know them again. She'd always loved the market when she was growing up. Many of the artists had been her very first mentors.

The sun warmed her skin as she quickly made her way to Miss Maple's booth. The older woman had her curly gray hair pinned on top of her head and was wearing thick, plastic-framed glasses, a corset, and a peasant skirt. Her lace-up, knee-high boots completed the outfit.

Abby strolled up to the booth and waited patiently while Miss Maple charmed a beautiful little girl by waving her hand over a row of cupcakes, changing the icing from blue to pink. Abby guessed the girl couldn't have been more than eight or nine years old.

"Can you make them purple?" the little girl asked, clapping her hands in excitement and making her dark curls bounce around her sweet face. "My mama's favorite color is purple."

"Demanding customer." Miss Maple winked at the girl and changed two of the cupcakes to purple.

"Yessssss." The girl's smile radiated up at Miss Maple, and Abby felt a kinship with her. Miss Maple had always been her favorite person in town, and it had all started with a pink cupcake.

"Go on," Miss Maple urged. "Take one for you and one for your mommy."

The girl hesitated for a moment, practically vibrating with anticipation. Then her lower lip jutted out in a slight pout as she pulled her pockets inside out. "I don't have any money."

Miss Maple leaned in and whispered, "Then it's your lucky day because the purple cupcakes are free. Go on. Take them. One for you, one for your mom."

The girl's face split into a huge grin, and then she grabbed one and took a giant bite, smearing purple icing all over her face.

"Olive!" A gorgeous blond woman scooted over and smacked the cupcake out of the girl's hand. "What do you think you're doing?"

Tears filled the girl's eyes, and she bowed her head, staring at her feet.

"You know you can't eat that. You have a shoot next week."

"Miss Maple gave it to me," the girl said, her voice wobbly with tears.

"Well, Miss Maple isn't the one who is going to have to worry about you fitting into the dress I just bought you, now is she?" The woman grabbed a handful of napkins and shoved them into the girl's hands. "Clean yourself up, Olive. If that food coloring stains your cheek who knows how long it will be before it fades. We can't afford for you to ruin the next shoot."

The woman turned on her heel and started to stalk off. Then she paused and glanced back at her daughter. "After you've cleaned up, meet me at the car. Your father is waiting."

Abby's mouth dropped open as she watched the woman disappear into the crowd, and she took a step forward, her hands lightly resting on the girl's shoulders as she crouched down. "Need some help, sweetheart?"

She shook her head, one fat tear standing in her big eyes as she bravely tried not to cry.

Abby gently took the tissues from her hand and cleaned the purple frosting from her face, dabbing at the tear she hadn't been able to hold back. She gave her a gentle smile. "There you go, pretty girl, all cleaned up."

"Abby? Olive?" Clay's unmistakable voice came from behind her.

"Daddy!" The girl let out a wail and flew past Abby.

Abby turned around to find Olive swept up in Clay's arms, her head on his shoulder as she clung to him.

"Hey, sweetheart. What's wrong?" he asked, staring over her shoulder at Abby. "Where's your mother?"

Olive shook her head and clung tighter.

Abby cleared her throat. "I think she's waiting in the car."

Clay's face turned stormy. "She left Olive here by herself?"

"She wasn't by herself, Clay," Miss Maple said, reaching over to pat him on the shoulder. "Abby and I were here."

He glanced from Miss Maple to Abby and back again then nodded. "Thanks."

Abby stood there, her heart nearly exploding with both tenderness and pain. Seeing him with his daughter, a daughter from another woman, was a gut punch she hadn't seen coming. She knew he'd had a child with his ex, she just hadn't ever seen her before, and Abby's reaction was visceral. And after seeing the way her mother had treated her only moments before, it made Abby want to wrap the little girl in her arms and keep her safe from the wicked witch.

Clay put his daughter on her feet and crouched down just as Abby had. "I missed you, bug."

Olive's lips curved into a whisper of a smile. "I missed you, too."

He nodded and hugged her again. "When did you two get back into town?"

"Last night."

"Last night?" His eyebrows shot up his forehead. "Where did you stay?"

"The Book and Stone. Mommy said it was too late to go home."

Clay ground his teeth, clearly annoyed, but he didn't say anything. He just nodded and grabbed her hand. "Let's go tell her goodbye, okay?"

Olive's face took on the same stormy expression Clay had worn just a few moments ago as she crossed her arms over her chest.

He narrowed his eyes. "What happened, bug?"

Her gaze shifted to the purple cupcake on the ground, but again just like her father, she didn't say anything.

What a pair they are, Abby thought. Both trying to shield the other from Olive's mother's behavior.

"What happened, Abby?" Clay asked.

Way to put me on the spot, Clay. Abby glanced once at Miss Maple then back at Clay. "There was a cupcake incident. I think Olive's mom didn't think it was a good idea."

Miss Maple snorted. "She definitely didn't approve."

Clay's gaze went to the cupcake still on the ground. His body tensed, and his face pinched with pain as he clearly put two and two together. He brushed one of her curls behind Olive's ear. "What do you say we make your favorite pie when we get home?"

Olive shook her head. "It's okay, Dad. I'm not supposed to be eating sweets anyway."

Her tone was so flat and emotionless it made Abby's heart nearly break. Before her mother showed up, Olive had been full of pure joy. Her mom had sucked the life right out of her daughter.

Miss Maple shook her head. "Now that's where I have to disagree, little lady. Where do you think the sweetness inside here comes from?" She pressed her palm to her heart as she glanced up at Clay and winked. "I'm going to have to insist you at least take a cookie."

Olive hesitated then looked to her dad for approval.

"It's okay, sweetheart. Go ahead," he said.

That exuberant smile broke out on her face again, and she reached for the cookie. As her fingers brushed over Miss Maple's, a tiny spark of magic flittered over her fingers.

Olive let out a giggle. "That tickled."

Miss Maple crooked her finger at her, indicating for Olive to lean in, and then whispered something in her ear.

Olive's giggle turned into a gasp, and she stared at Miss Maple with wide, excited eyes. "Really?"

Miss Maple nodded. "Really. Enjoy, Olive. Come see me next week, okay?"

"I will." She flashed her dimples and grabbed her dad's hand as she took a big bite of the cookie.

"Thank you, Miss Maple," Clay said then he turned to Abby. "You, too, Abs."

"I didn't do anything," she said. "No need to thank me."

He paused, holding her gaze for a beat. "Yes, you did. Thanks."

Emotion rose up and clogged her throat. She swallowed and said, "Anytime, Clay." Smiling at Olive she put her hand out. "We didn't get a chance to meet. I'm Abby."

"Olive," Clay's daughter said around another mouthful of cookie and quickly shook Abby's hand.

"Nice to meet you, Olive. See you around."

Olive waved and then tugged on Clay's hand, her steps bouncy as she led him away from the booth.

Abby watched them go, her heart aching for all that could've been had she stayed in Keating Hollow ten years ago.

"He's not lost, you know," Miss Maple said.

"Huh?"

"Clay. He's been through a lot, but so have you. With time comes wisdom, but you have to be open enough to put yourself out there."

Abby shook her head, her insides churning with regret. "I appreciate what you're trying to say, but that's not going to happen. It can't."

Miss Maple tilted her head to the side and studied Abby. "Why not? No path is predetermined."

"Because I can't stay," Abby blurted. She already knew if she started dating Clay, she'd fall head-over-heels for him again. Leaving him again would kill her. Then there was Olive. Clay's situation had suddenly become all too real. He had a daughter he obviously adored, and that little girl already had a grip on Abby's heart after five minutes. She couldn't get attached to them and then walk out of their lives. But more importantly, it wasn't fair to Clay or Olive.

"I see," Miss Maple said. "Have you ever asked yourself why you keep running, Abby?"

"I don't need to," Abby said hotly.

Miss Maple raised her eyebrows. "Are you sure about that?"

"I'm sure."

Miss Maple nodded, but sadness crept into her hazel eyes. "I understand why you left. Pain is a powerful motivator, but you can't keep it locked away forever. Running doesn't make it go away; it only helps it fester."

Abby's entire body went cold as she remembered Charlotte's still body lying in her shed, her unseeing eyes staring at nothing. The memory made Abby blanch, and she quickly shook her head. "I'm not keeping it locked away. It's always right here." Abby pointed to her heart. "So please, I know you're trying to help, but I'm not running. I'm just trying to survive."

Miss Maple reached out. "Abby—"

"No." Abby jerked back. "I have to go. It was nice to see you again." Then she turned and ran out of the market, tears streaming silently down her face.

CHAPTER 12

Olive pointed to the sleek Mercedes rental car parked at the far end of the parking lot. "It's that one."

Of course it is, Clay thought. His ex-wife always did have a taste for the finer things in life, and he'd had the credit card bills to prove it. Budgeting wasn't one of her strong suits. Clay tightened his grip on his daughter's hand and walked up to the car.

Val, who was sitting in the driver's seat, put her hand up, indicating for him to wait. Her mouth was moving and he guessed she was on a call. Her laugh tinkled through the window, and he rolled his eyes. That fake laugh never failed to get his hackles up. He'd heard it far too many times when she was trying to manipulate her way into something.

"Daddy, look!" Olive called from a few feet away. His daughter was bent at the knees, inspecting something on the ground.

"What is it, sweet girl?" he asked, moving toward her, his irritation fading into the background. Olive never failed to lift his spirits. She was curious, kindhearted, and rambunctious enough to keep him on his toes. Life with her was always going to be an adventure.

"It's a penny." She sat down and crossed her legs as she held it up with two fingers. "I bet it's magical. Make a wish."

Clay smiled down at her. "You know, I bet you're right. But why don't you do the honors? You're the one who found it."

She beamed, squeezed her eyes closed, and moved her lips in a silent request. He could guess what she was wishing for. It was the same thing she always wished for—a puppy. Clay had been trying to hold out until her birthday, but that was over two months away. He wasn't sure he was going to make it.

When Olive opened her eyes, they were sparkling, and she said, "I'm going to name her Endora."

"From *Bewitched*?" Clay asked. "I thought you were leaning toward Sabrina."

"I was, but Endora makes me laugh." She shrugged. "Do you think the puppy would mind blue eyeshadow?"

"Olive, you can't put makeup on a dog," Val said disapprovingly from behind them. "Now get up. You're getting your clothes dirty."

Clay held out a hand for his daughter, helping her to her feet. He couldn't help but notice his playful, outgoing daughter had vanished and was at once replaced with one who was sullen and wouldn't look at her mother. He squeezed her hand, silently giving her support.

"Look at what you did to those new pants. Olive, how many times have I told you, you have to take care of your things?"

"I'm sorry, Mommy," Olive said, sounding more like she was four or five instead of eight.

"You should be. I can't take you to bookings looking like that."

"About that," Clay said, narrowing his eyes at his ex. "I don't think it's a good idea for Olive to be involved in any more shoots until she gets a little older."

"Clay." Val shook her head. "It's not up to you to decide what she does while we're together."

"The hell it isn't," he said, swallowing the urge to yell at her. "If Olive is going to work in Hollywood, it's absolutely something we should be discussing." He glanced down at his daughter. "Want to tell me about the shoot you just had?"

Olive shrugged one shoulder but didn't say anything.

That wasn't a good sign. Olive never held back when she enjoyed something. Her exuberance came in the form of nonstop talking and scheming about when she'd be able to do it again. It was obvious whatever had happened down in Palm Springs, Olive wasn't a fan.

"Val?" he asked. "What did you and Olive do these last couple of weeks?"

"I told you already, Clay. We had a shoot. A commercial. They wanted Olive to play a birthday girl. I thought it'd be fun. Why not? And besides, it's a great way to get her started. The more she learns about filming, the better it will be during pilot season."

"Pilot season? Now wait just—"

"I have to go, Clay," she said and opened her arms for Olive. "Give me a hug, sweetheart."

Olive did as her mother asked, and although she hugged Val tightly, Clay couldn't help noticing she let go quickly and attached herself to his side, holding on as if he was her lifeline.

"I'll see you next week, Olive. And remember, no sweets."

Olive stiffened and held on tighter to Clay.

"Next week?" Clay asked, rubbing his hand on Olive's shoulder. "What do you mean by that? Her next school break isn't until the winter solstice."

"We have an audition, Clay. I already got her a ticket. All

you have to do is put her on the plane. I'll be there at LAX to pick her up. It's just a quick four days then she'll be back. You can get her homework from her teachers."

Clay blinked at her. Then he shook his head. "No, Val. I'm not going to allow her to miss school for some Hollywood dream that she doesn't even want."

Val took a step forward. "You don't know what she wants. You haven't even asked her. And I'm not gonna let you take away her dreams just because you don't like that I chose to have a career over you."

Clay's mouth dropped open in surprise as he took in her words. Was she being serious? Judging by the indignant expression on her face, she was dead serious. He cleared his throat. "I think it would be best if we talk about this later after we've both had some time to think it over."

"You can talk all you want to, Clay, but you're not stopping our daughter from doing this. Doors are opening for her, and I won't let you tank her shot. Put her on the plane. I'll email you her ticket."

"No." Clay stood his ground. He wasn't putting his eight-year-old daughter on a plane by herself.

Val's eyes narrowed. "You will, or I'll sue for custody."

Anger coiled through him as he stared at his ex. He knew she wasn't bluffing, and to be honest it scared the hell out of him. But he also knew without even asking that Olive wasn't interested in whatever her mother was trying to push on her, and he wouldn't let Val force Olive into a life she didn't want. "Do what you have to do, Val. We'll let the lawyers sort it out."

"You'll regret this, Clay." Val sent him a venomous look then slammed the Mercedes into gear and sped out of the parking lot.

"I probably will," he muttered as he watched the sleek black car disappear around a corner.

SOUL OF THE WITCH

"Dad?"

He glanced down at Olive. "Yes, love?"

"I can go with mom if she wants," she said meekly. "I can do better next time."

He kneeled in front of his daughter. "What do you mean 'do better next time?'"

She let out a sigh, and her face flushed pink as she glanced away.

"Olive?" He reached up and gently turned her face so that she was forced to look at him. "Please tell me what happened."

Tears sprang in her big brown eyes and she sniffed. "Mom wanted to go to an audition and instead of staying with her smelly neighbor, I begged to go along."

"Because you wanted to be in it?" Clay asked, trying to figure out when his daughter had decided acting was her passion.

Olive shook her head. "I didn't want to stay with the smelly neighbor. Her apartment always smells like rotting fish."

Clay wrinkled his nose. "Can't say I blame you."

She rewarded him with a shy smile. "It was really boring."

"I bet. How did you end up in the shoot?"

She shrugged. "They asked me to audition and Mom wanted me to, so I did. Then they cast me, but not her." Olive chewed on her lower lip. "I think Mom was mad at me."

He didn't doubt for a minute that was true. For Val, the idea of someone, much less her daughter, stealing the spotlight was unthinkable. Her jealousy was probably eating her from the inside out. "Mom was probably just disappointed you both weren't chosen, sweetheart."

She shrugged, clearly not buying his crap.

"Well, did you have fun at least?" he asked.

"No. It was cold."

Getting information from her was like squeezing juice

from a raisin. "I thought you were in Palm Springs. Isn't it warm there right now?"

She nodded, her eyes glazing over as her voice shook. "But it's cold at night in the pool."

Dammit. Clay wanted to hit something. They'd made her go in the pool. How could Val have put her daughter through that? No wonder Olive hadn't enjoyed herself. She was afraid of water and had been ever since she'd slipped off a rock at the beach and gotten sucked under by the waves. Clay had been right there, diving in to save her. But the churn had been strong, and Olive had hit her head on the rock, causing her to black out. She'd been terrified ever since. "That doesn't sound like fun at all," he said, trying his best to not feed her fear.

She shook her head.

"Listen, Olive. I need you to tell me something. Are you interested in doing commercials with your mom? Do you like acting?"

His girl's eyes filled with tears as she slowly shook her head.

"It's okay, baby," he said gently. "You don't have to do them ever again if you don't want to."

"But M—Mom will b—be mad," she stuttered, her little body shaking with her sobs.

He couldn't hate Val. She was the mother of his child, the child who was the center of his world. But in that moment, he wished she'd walk back out of their lives. She'd hurt Olive either way, he was sure of it, but at least he'd be able keep his girl safe from the world Val was determined to live in. "She'll be fine," he said, stroking her hair. "I'll talk to her. You don't need to worry about anything."

"Do I h—have to go b—back next week?" She sounded so dejected it nearly broke Clay's heart. "I want to stay h—here."

"No. You don't have to go. You have school, and that's important." He held her for a few more minutes until she calmed down. Then he pulled back and wiped her tears just as Abby had done earlier when he'd spotted them together. "How about we go get some lunch?"

"Can we have ice cream after?" she asked, her eyes lighting up.

"Didn't you already have a cookie?" he asked, already knowing the answer.

"That wasn't dessert. It was a Happy Cookie."

He squinted at her. "What's a Happy Cookie?"

She grinned and clapped her hands. Suddenly she was holding a yellow frosted sugar cookie just like the one Miss Maple had given her earlier. "This. Miss Maple said they're magic."

They certainly were. Clay hadn't missed the spark of magic Miss Maple had bestowed upon his little girl, and now he knew their secret. She'd given Olive the ability to summon her cookies at will. He chuckled to himself, knowing Val would lose her mind. He grinned. "If you're going to stuff yourself with cookies, I don't think you're going to have room for ice cream."

"No, silly." She giggled and pressed it into his hand. "It's for you. It's supposed to make you happy."

He didn't need a cookie when he had his beautiful daughter smiling up at him, but he took a bite anyway and said, "Never been happier."

CHAPTER 13

*A*bby sat in her dad's truck in front of Charming Herbals, her hands still gripping the steering wheel. She was shaken from the memory of Charlotte's death. It was an event she never let herself think about, and the reason she rarely stepped foot in Keating Hollow. She knew Miss Maple was just trying to help, but it wasn't help she could use.

Charlotte's death wasn't anything Abby was running from. She took full responsibility and would live with what had happened forever, but she couldn't live with the memory in the forefront of her mind day in and day out. Not on a regular basis anyway. Three months was the deal she'd made with herself. She'd stay for three months until her dad was out of the woods, and then she'd go back to New Orleans. If her dad wasn't out of the woods, she'd get a place on the coast within driving distance so she could be available when he needed her. But staying in Keating Hollow... no. That was out of the question.

A sharp knock on the truck's window startled her out of

her thoughts, and she let out a gasp as she jumped. With her heart in her throat, she rolled the window down. "Noel. Hi."

Noel leaned down, her red hair falling over one eye. "What are you doing just sitting here?"

"Just... taking a second before I go in." She forced a bright smile. "You picking up a few things?"

She nodded. "I'm going to smudge Dad's place for him. Clear out any negative energy." Her gaze swept over Abby as she frowned. "Speaking of negative energy, what the heck have you been up to today? Your aura is murky as hell. You should probably ask Bree for a cleanse before you go home and infect Dad with whatever you've got going on."

Abby gritted her teeth, hating that her sister was probably right. She hated that her mood most likely did affect her dad, and she was irritated she hadn't thought of it already. "Fine. I'll ask her."

"Good." She pulled the door open. "Come on. Daisy's waiting inside."

A smile tugged at Abby's lips at the mention of her niece. "Just the person to brighten my spirits. How is my favorite girl today?"

Noel led the way to the front door of the shop. "Ask her yourself."

The bell rang above the door as Abby slipped inside the cozy shop. Twinkle lights lit up the wooden shelves lining the walls filled with various herbs, crystals, and other ingredients. A pair of overstuffed couches sat in the middle of the store where customers were welcome to sit and browse through the many spells Bree kept on hand. Off to the right there was a small café that specialized in restorative teas. And in the back was a small work area where Bree whipped up various custom potions.

"Good afternoon, ladies," Bree said from behind the

checkout counter. She wiped her hands on the apron she wore over her jeans and T-shirt and waved. A piece of her dark hair fell from her bun, and Bree blew it out of her face as she grinned at them. "Let me know if I can help you find anything."

"We will," Noel said.

Abby waved at Bree, a woman she'd known all her life, then she turned her attention to Daisy, who immediately came running over.

"Auntie!" she cried and threw herself into Abby's arms.

Abby laughed and swung her around in a circle. "Hey you. What are you doing in here? Learning how to turn your enemies into toads?"

She giggled. "I prefer butterflies."

"Awe." Abby grinned and set her back down on her feet. "Your enemies should be so lucky."

"Mommy's going to show me how to make candles later." She held up a how-to book. "She says they will keep the bad spirits away."

"Wow. That sounds cool," Abby said and glanced over Daisy's shoulder, lifting one eyebrow in question.

Nightmares, Noel mouthed.

An ache formed in Abby's heart, and she wondered if Daisy's nightmares had anything to do with her father's disappearance. Daisy had been three when he'd walked out and never come back. Daisy had been the last person to see him. When Noel had gotten home, she'd found her daughter sitting on the couch, hugging a teddy bear, and crying. He'd told her he'd be right back, but as near as Noel could tell, her daughter had been home alone for more than three hours.

Abby reached out and squeezed Noel's hand. To her surprise, her sister squeezed back, but she quickly dropped Abby's hand and said, "We'll be over there picking out dyes for our candles."

Noel bent her head to her daughter's and whispered something. Daisy grinned and shot across the shop, laughing at whatever her mother had said. Abby watched the pair of them, her heart full of love and also a tiny bit of sadness. Between watching Clay with Olive and Noel with Daisy, she was starting to feel an ache deep in her chest. Growing up, she'd always thought she and Clay would stay in Keating Hollow, get married a few years out of high school, and start a family pretty soon after. In her imagined reality, she'd have a shop for her lotions here in town and be happily married with two kids, a dog, and backyard garden. Instead she was boyfriend-less and not sure where she'd be living in three months. She sighed and grabbed a handbasket.

Once Abby's basket was full of fresh herbs and plant-based fragrances, she set her loot on the counter and asked Bree, "Do you still make potions for nausea?"

"Sure. What's the cause?"

Abby grimaced. "It's for my dad. After his treatments."

Bree furrowed her brow and glanced at Noel. "Did he run out already?"

"Excuse me?" Abby asked. "Run out? He doesn't have anything other than what the nurse gave him."

"But—"

"He has all her potions, Abby," Noel said as she walked over to them. "I picked them up last week so he'd have them on hand."

"Then why isn't he using them?" Abby asked, confused. Her dad had been sick for two straight days. She couldn't understand why he was choosing to suffer his way through the aftermath of his chemo.

Noel let out a sigh. "Of course he's using them, Abby. They just aren't working the way we'd hoped."

"Chemotherapy is one heck of a poison for a reason," Bree

said. "I do my best, but my potions are only good for reducing symptoms. They don't eliminate them. And for some clients, they barely register in effectiveness. I'm sorry they aren't working better for your dad."

"It's not your fault," Noel said, and although she was talking to Bree, her eyes met Abby's. "You *tried*, and that's all we can ask."

Abby winced. The message was loud and clear. She hadn't even tried to make something that would ease her father's pain. Staring her sister in the eye she asked, "Why didn't you tell me?"

"Would it have made a difference?" Noel asked, tilting her head to the side, studying Abby.

"I could've at least made sure he was taking them," Abby said.

"He has been." Noel shook her head and raised her voice. "Don't you get it? He didn't tell you because he doesn't want you to feel guilty for not getting your butt out in the studio to make him the one thing he needs right now."

"I—"

"Save it, Abby. We all know you *can't* make your potions anymore. We've heard it a million times. What I don't get is how you manage to live with yourself, knowing Dad's suffering while you could do something about it."

Pressure weighed on Abby's chest as tears burned the backs of her eyes. Everything inside her screamed for her to make something to help her dad. But then in the same breath, everything shut down, and she was paralyzed in place.

Noel closed her eyes and shook her head. "I'll never understand you, Abby."

"I hope you never have to," Abby finally forced out. "Never have to put your magic in a box and lock it up because you're afraid of what it will do."

"You know, Abs, if that's what you'd actually done all these years, I'd understand. But we both know that isn't the case." She turned her back on Abby, pulled out her wallet, and handed Bree her credit card for her candle making supplies.

After she signed her credit card slip, Noel reached her hand out to Daisy and said, "Say goodbye to your aunt, Daisy."

"Bye, Auntie." Daisy wrapped her arms around Abby's waist and squeezed her tight before letting go. "See you later!"

Abby waved as she watched them leave, and then she slumped against the counter.

"Are you all right?" Bree asked her.

"Honestly," Abby said, "I have no idea." She shook her head and gave Bree a pained look. "Can you add an energy cleanse, fennel, cinnamon, and cumin to my order? And some binding crystals."

"You're sure?" Bree asked, knowing exactly what Abby wanted the herbs for.

Abby let out a huff of humorless laughter. "No. Not at all. But you heard my sister. I have to try, don't I?"

Bree nodded. "Give me a sec." She disappeared into her storeroom while Abby clutched the counter, her knuckles turning white with the idea of making a potion for her dad. What if she messed it up again? What if the potion made his symptoms worse? What if he had a reaction and... She shook her head hard, unwilling to go down that path again. This time would be different. For her dad, it would be different.

"Here we go," Bree said, striding back to the counter. "I also added some ginger and lemongrass. If nothing seems to work, consider bringing him in for some acupuncture. I have some special needles that might do the trick."

"Thanks, Bree. I appreciate it."

"You're welcome," she said, placing the items in a canvas

bag. "If there's anything else I can do to help, you know where to find me."

Abby paid for her items, and with her heart pounding against her breast bone, she left the shop and headed for the brewery and her new work studio.

CHAPTER 14

The afternoon light flooded through the window of the small brew shed, shining on the boxes lining the wall. Abby set her supplies on the stainless steel counter and blew out a long breath. She had to settle herself or this would never work, and she wouldn't even be able to get her soap recipes right.

The only thing to do was put her dad, his illness, and the nausea potion out of her mind while she got to work on her inventory. Then, once she was in her groove, she'd revisit the idea of making something for her dad. Just the thought of it made her hands shake. She slammed her notebook down on the counter and shook her head.

No, she would not let her anxiety get the better of her. Not today. Not in this place that was full of her dad's positive energy. It was as if she could feel him in the room, and it made her warm inside. Remembering simpler days when she'd watched him work up his batches of brew, she went to work on putting away her supplies.

It wasn't long before she was standing in front of the stove, stirring her soap mixture and getting ready to add her special ingredients. Making soap was easy. Anyone could do it, really. But Abby's line was unique because she infused them with earth elements that helped the skin stay soft and youthful. Today she was working with primrose seeds. She held them in the palm of her hand, the weight of them familiar and soothing to her soul. That faint whisper of magic she'd become so good at manipulating tingled over her fingers and soaked into the primrose, making the seeds glow for just a moment.

There. Perfect. She sprinkled them into the pot and stirred. The current of magic lit up the soap mixture then zapped out, indicating the batch was ready. Humming, Abby poured the soap into the waiting molds, set it on the portable rack, and moved on to another batch.

Hours slipped away while Abby immersed herself in her work, and by the time all of her soap molds were filled and she'd bottled a half dozen batches of lotions, the sun had set and her stomach was rumbling. She glanced over at the nausea potion ingredients Bree had gathered for her and decided she'd better eat first. It wouldn't pay to be lightheaded when she tapped her magic again, especially since it would take a great deal more power than she was used to utilizing.

After removing her apron, Abby stepped out of the brewery shed and made her way into the pub. Chatter rose up around her as she took a seat at the end of the bar. She glanced around, noting the place was packed and the staff bustling from table to table.

"Come to give us a hand?" Rhys asked, placing a glass of ice water in front of Abby.

She turned back around. "If you need help, sure."

He waved a hand and shook his head. "Nah. We've got it under control. Just giving you a hard time. Want to order something?"

"Yes. I've been working all day in the brew shed and I'm starving. California burger and garlic fries."

He raised an eyebrow. "Living dangerously, I see."

She laughed. "Just making sure I'm prepared for any random vampire attack."

"Riiight." He reached for a glass and nodded to the taps. "What's your poison tonight?"

"None for me. Still have work to do." If she was going to try her hand at a potion, she couldn't risk being even slightly tipsy. "How about a root beer float?"

A smile split across his face as he noted her choices. "I love a girl who's not afraid to enjoy her meal."

"I've got no one to impress." Abby shrugged. "Might as well live a little."

"What about what's-his-name back in New Orleans?" Clay's unmistakable voice sounded in her ear, sending a shiver down her spine.

She turned slowly and eyed him. He was wearing a steel blue, button-down shirt, dark jeans, and scuffed cowboy boots. Her fingers twitched, aching to caress his stubbled jawline. Damn, he was gorgeous. He possessed a quiet, rugged hotness that was obvious to everyone but him. "No what's-his-name. That appears to be over."

His playful smile vanished, and concern flashed through his dark eyes. "Are you okay?"

Abby waved a dismissive hand. "Fine. It's been a long time coming. Turns out he's an ass and it took me putting my family first for his true colors to really show."

Clay sat on the stool next to her and grabbed her hand, squeezing it lightly before he let go. "I've been there."

Abby wondered if he was talking about Val, but didn't want to ask. What she'd seen of his ex that morning was quite enough. "It happens, I guess. But"—she smiled brightly—"I'm relieved it's done, so moving forward, right?" Rhys arrived with her root beer float and a porter for Clay. Abby thanked him and raised her drink in a toast. "To a new start."

Clay gave her a whisper of a smile as he grabbed his beer and touched his glass to hers. "To a new start."

Abby met Clay's gaze and held it as she took a sip of her root beer. A profound intensity passed between them, something that seemed deeper than anything they'd shared when they were kids. Abby had a strange feeling that in some cosmic way, their life experiences had led them both to this exact moment.

Clay glanced away, clearing his throat as he placed his beer back on the bar and signaled for Rhys.

"What's up, boss?" he asked. "Need dinner?"

"Yeah. Burger and fries should do it."

"Anything for Olive?"

Clay shook his head. "She's at a friend's birthday party, no doubt consuming enough food for three days."

"Lucky her." Rhys retreated to place Clay's order, and even though the pub still buzzed with the loud din of diners, a silence fell between Abby and Clay.

Abby stared down at the ice cream melting in her root beer float and wished desperately for a beer of her own, anything to settle her nerves that were suddenly jumping all over the place. She didn't know what to say to Clay. Everything that she wanted to ask wasn't any of her business, and everything that was going on in her life was too personal to bring up in the middle of the pub. She didn't want the staff to know her dad was having trouble with the treatments. He deserved to maintain his image of the strong man they'd come to know and love.

"Thank you," Clay said, staring straight ahead at the clock on the wall. "For being there for Olive this morning, I mean."

"I didn't do anything, Clay."

"Yeah, you did, and I want you to know how much I appreciate it."

She turned and gave him a gentle smile. "You're welcome. She's a sweet girl. Beautiful, too. I don't know how she doesn't have you wrapped around her little finger."

He snorted. "Who said she doesn't?"

Abby laughed. "Well that makes sense."

Their food showed up, and while they ate Clay launched into an animated story about how Olive had conned him into a rabbit that ended up having babies two days later. He told story after story that highlighted a rambunctious little girl with a giant heart. By the time he was done, Abby was more than a little bit in love with his daughter.

"She sounds wonderful, Clay. You might have your hands full, but I'd say you hit the lottery with that one."

"She *is* wonderful, and you're right on both counts. She sure makes life interesting."

Abby stood, grateful he'd chosen to regale her with Olive stories. He'd kept her entertained and relaxed while she ate her dinner, and now she felt better than she had all day. "Thanks for the company. It's was nice chatting with you on my dinner break."

"Any time, Abs." He glanced around. "Dinner break? Are you picking up a shift or something?"

"Or something. I've been working out in the old brew shed all day. Time to get back to it." She threw a generous tip on the bar. "See you around."

"Sure," he said, frowning slightly as he got up and shoved his hands in his pockets. "It was nice seeing you, Abby."

She placed her hand on his arm for just a moment then slipped out of the pub and back into the shed. Leaning her back against the closed door, Abby let out a sigh. How was it possible she'd ever left that man? He was everything she'd thought he'd turn out to be. And the way he talked about his daughter… She pressed her hand to her rapidly beating heart, waiting for it to return to normal.

"Okay, Abby, time to get it together." She pushed herself off the door and grabbed the ingredients she'd picked up at Bree's. The potion wasn't hard to make, it just required precision and timing. After digging out her copper sauce pan, Abby filled it with distilled water and placed it on the stove on low heat. Then she moved to the counter and minced the fennel, cinnamon, and cumin before she transferred it to the mortar and used the pestle to make a smooth paste.

Steam started to rise from the copper pan, and suddenly it was the moment of truth. Time to see what she was made of. Abby scooped the paste out of the mortar, let her power concentrate in the palm of her hand and started to chant. "Heal thy body. Revive thy spirit. Let the Earth restore thy strength."

A magical light flashed, illuminating the brewing shed and nearly blinding Abby with its intensity. She couldn't see it, but she sensed her magic settling into the herbs. The moment her palm started to tingle, she held her hand over the pan and scraped the paste into the simmering water.

Sparks of light shot up from the steam billowing out of the pan, and Abby smiled. Yes. That was exactly what was supposed to happen. She grabbed her wooden spoon and started to stir, careful to keep the mixture from boiling. When the paste was completely incorporated, she grabbed the fresh lemons from her bag of tricks and added a generous amount of lemon juice to the potion. Her concoction started to bubble, and Abby removed it from the heat. As it started to cool down, she held the wooden spoon still, using it as a conduit, and said, "From bone to earth and earth to bone, may this healing potion be the center stone."

Magic in the form of white light curled around the wooden spoon and seeped into the potion. It immediately turned sunset orange, exactly as she'd intended. Abby grinned, relief rushing through her. She'd done it.

She reached for an empty plastic bottle, but before she could transfer the potion to the bottle, it suddenly curdled and turned a sickly green color. "What the…"

She lifted the mixture and sniffed. "Oh, no. Gross."

Frustrated, she poured the entire mixture down the drain. Once the copper pot was scrubbed, she set her shoulders and tried again.

Two hours and four batches later, Abby was low on ingredients and completely out of patience. Every single time, no matter if she changed equipment or the timing, the potion turned the same putrid green and smelled like the inside of a used sneaker.

"What am I doing wrong?" she yelled and threw the wooden spoon across the shed. It clattered to the ground, bounced twice, and stilled. Abby scowled. It was as if the wooden spoon was mocking her, just lying there innocuously as if it had done nothing wrong.

A knock sounded on the door, followed by Clay's worried voice. "Abby? Are you okay in there?"

She flung the door open. "No. I'm not okay. I'm not even close to okay." All the emotion she'd been holding back while trying to make a potion she hadn't made for ten years came rushing to the surface. She turned, retreated to the counter, and slumped forward, holding her head in her hands. "My magic is broken. I rejected it, so it rejected me!"

Clay stepped through the door and quietly made his way to the work station. Peeking into the copper pan, he grimaced and said, "What happened?"

Abby dropped her hands and stared blankly at the wall. "I have no idea."

"What were you trying to make?"

She turned, her eyes pinched with pain. "A potion to help with my dad's nausea."

"Oh." The word came out in a whisper.

There was no need for Abby to explain what a big deal it was that she was even trying such a thing. He'd been there ten years ago when everything had gone sideways when she'd been trying to help Charlotte.

Clay straightened his shoulders and said, "The only way to figure this out is to walk through it step by step."

"I already did that," she said stubbornly.

"With a second set of eyes? Have you let anyone analyze what might be going wrong?"

"No."

He gave her a mildly impatient look. "Come on, Abs. You know as well as I do that sometimes we're too close to a potion or recipe to see where things are going wrong. Let me shadow you while you try one more batch."

"It's no use. Obviously healing potions aren't my calling. That was made crystal clear ten years ago." She stared at him, practically daring him to challenge her.

He crossed his arms over his chest, studying her as if he was trying to decide if it was worth it to argue.

"Bring it on, Garrison. Everyone else has weighed in. Why not you?" She was itching for a fight and needed to vent her frustration. And even though she knew he didn't deserve her wrath, he was the one who was directly in her path. "Spit it out."

He let out a small snort of derision. "You don't want to hear what I have to say."

"Really?" she asked, irritated at his less-than-supportive attitude. "Try me. Go on. I'm waiting."

"If you're sure..."

"I'm sure, dammit," she yelled, her fists balled at her side as she let go of the last bits of her control. "What is it you've been holding back for the last ten years? Tell me exactly what you think of me. How I hurt you and everyone around me and... and..." A sob clogged her throat and she couldn't get out the words that she'd been holding in for as long as she could remember.

Clay took a step forward and wrapped Abby in his arms. She stiffened, holding her arms together in front of her chest as a sort of shield from his love and support. But that didn't stop her from resting her head on his shoulder as her body was racked by silent sobs.

"Shh, Abby. It wasn't your fault." He stroked her long blond hair, whispering over and over again. "Charlotte was sick. Very sick. You have to stop doing this to yourself."

She shook her head almost violently. "The potion should've made her stronger. Instead, it put her in a coma and the next thing I knew..." She didn't finish the sentence. She couldn't. The images were there, right in the forefront of her mind. Her best friend, who'd been counting on her, was gone.

"You have to find a way to let this go, Abby," he said gently. "Charlotte wouldn't want you to hold on to this for forever."

She knew he was right and had told herself the same thing a million times before. But being back in Keating Hollow and trying to process her dad's illness, it was too much. And now that she couldn't even make a simple potion that had been second nature all those years ago, she just felt broken. "I know," she finally said, pulling away and wiping her eyes. "It's just that with my dad's diagnosis and not being able to get this damn potion right, I can't seem to keep myself together."

He glanced in the pan again. "How about we try it together? Let me see if I can help."

She hesitated, not sure she could focus after her outburst.

"Come on, Abs. Who better than another earth witch to evaluate your witchin' skills?" He grinned at her and raised his eyebrows in challenge.

That cocky, playful look on his face reminded her of simpler days when life hadn't yet dealt them a plateful of heartache and disappointment, when they'd pushed each other to learn to be better, more skilled witches. It was the memory of their innocence and optimism more than anything else that prompted her to say, "Okay, Garrison. But I'm warning you now. I've tried everything I can think of, so you've got your work cut out for you."

His grin widened. "Bring it on, Townsend."

Abby went through each of the steps just as she had before, while Clay stood off to the side observing. He was so quiet and she was concentrating so hard that she completely forgot he was there when she finally tapped her magic again and said, "From bone to earth and earth to bone, may this healing potion be the center stone."

The magic behaved just as she expected it to, and once again when she was done, the liquid turned putrid green. She threw up her hands and turned to Clay. "I can't keep doing this. Either the ingredients are bad or my power is tainted."

"I don't think it's the ingredients," he said.

"Great. So it is me. I knew it." She started collecting the various utensils and shoved them into the pot. Her movements were agitated, and because she was afraid she'd start crying again, she added, "You probably need to get going. I don't want to keep you."

"I don't have anywhere to be." Clay took the copper pan and

rinsed the failed potion down the drain. "There's no rush to get home. Olive is still with her friends."

Abby grabbed a clean towel and her all-natural citrus cleaner and went to work wiping down the counter. "Okay, but you certainly don't need to be doing my dishes. Go on, Clay. Go have a beer or something. I'm sure hanging out with your crazy ex wasn't exactly on your to-do list."

He chuckled. "You just let me handle what's on my to-do list. In the meantime, let's talk about why your execution keeps falling short when it comes to that potion."

"Because my magic is cursed?" she asked flippantly.

Clay finished washing the copper pan and set it aside before turning to face her. "No, Abby, it's not cursed at all. But I do think you're either holding back or your magic is blocked."

She shook her head, frustrated with his conclusion. "Neither of those things are true. I'm putting everything I have into this, and my magic is there, it's just not cooperating on *this* spell. I can still make my soaps and lotions without any issues."

"Soaps and lotions that require far less skill and precision," he said as if she wasn't already aware her skincare products used minimal power.

"So?"

"You don't need everything you've got to make those. But for a healing potion? It's a different story. And if you ask me, the power you were giving off... pretty weak, to be honest. Next time, dig deeper. This isn't a time to be cautious."

"I was digging deep," she mumbled. "All it got me was a pukey sludge."

He finished the dishes and turned around, watching her as she packed up her potion-making tools. When she was finally done and just standing there, unsure of what to do with herself, he said, "I think you should talk to someone about what happened."

Her face burned with heat, and everything in her shut down. "I'm not going down this road again, Clay. Thanks for the help, but we're done here." He opened his mouth to say something, but she reached for the door and swept her arm out, indicating it was time for him to leave. "I don't want to talk about this. Good night, Clay."

He stood there staring at her for a few beats, but then he finally nodded. "I'm going. But first, promise me you'll look into ways to unblock your gift?"

Abby shook her head. "I don't think so, Clay. It's... it never works."

"If there was something that might work, would you try it?"

She hesitated. It was a good question. Everything about her magic was a rough road to travel. Memories, disappointments, heartache. She really didn't want to relive any of it, but for her dad, she'd do what she had to do. "Yeah, I guess I would."

"I'm going to hold you to that," he said, his lips splitting into a pleased smile as he pointed a finger at her. "Don't think I won't."

"Oh, no chance of that," Abby said and all but shoved him out of the shed. Once he was gone, she gathered her things and tapped out a text to Noel.

I tried. Many times. All of the batches failed. I'm sorry.

CHAPTER 15

*T*he lunch rush had just died down when Clay made his way into his office. He'd already spent far too much time behind the bar that week, more than usual. He'd told Rhys it was because Sadie was still out nursing her wounds. She'd ended up with two deep gashes that had needed more stitches than he could count, and she was under strict orders to not lift anything over a couple pounds until the flesh started to heal.

But filling in for Sadie hadn't been the only reason he'd spent more time in the pub. If he was honest, it hadn't even been the main reason. The other servers, along with Rhys, were more than capable of picking up the slack. But every time Clay holed up in his office, he found himself itching to get back out into the restaurant where he spent the majority of his time staring at the front doors and waiting for a certain blonde to walk back into the pub.

Of course, she hadn't. He hadn't seen her since she'd tossed him out of the brew shed a few nights ago. She hadn't even shown up to make more of her soaps and lotions, at least not while he'd been around. Her absence was driving him insane. Now that he knew she no longer had a significant other, he couldn't get her out of his mind. When he'd had his arms around her, he'd felt things he hadn't felt in a very long time. He wanted to protect her, be there for her, love her.

"Stop," he muttered to himself and focused on the notes he'd written for his current beer recipe. He wrote *Winter Brew Holiday Ale* on the top of the sheet and went to work on calculating the ingredient conversions for a large batch.

"Clay?" Rhys said, after a short knock on his opened door. "Don't mean to interrupt, but there's someone here to see you."

Abby. But even as he dropped the pen and stood, he knew his assessment was wrong. If Abby was there and wanted to see him, Rhys would've just sent her back, and he certainly wouldn't have referred to her as 'someone.'

"Who is it?" Clay asked, following Rhys into the front of the house.

"No idea. But she's pretty enough." His assistant flashed him an appreciative smile. "Why does it seem like you've put a spell on all the hotties in town? Do you spike their brew or something?"

"Or something," Clay said truthfully. He actually did spell the beer... or at least the ingredients. But as far as he could tell, his efforts had never resulted in a love spell, thank the gods. "It's probably more my sparkling personality."

Rhys snorted his reply and pointed to a woman at the end of the bar. She was wearing a formfitting suit and had her hair swept up in a fancy twist. Gold cuffs encircled one wrist and a matching pendant was displayed just above her cleavage.

Expensive was the word that came to mind when Clay assessed her. Vender? Sales rep? Marketing exec trying to get a piece of the Keating Hollow Brewery money train? It didn't matter. He was the one in charge, and he was the one who had to deal with her.

Clay made his way over to the woman and placed his hands on the bar. "What can I do for you today?"

She looked him up and down as if assessing him then said, "Clayton Garrison?"

"Yes."

She reached into her messenger bag and pulled out an envelope. "You've been served. Have a nice day."

Clay clutched the envelope, staring after her as she breezed out of the bar. Then the anger set in. There was only one person who'd be suing him. Gritting his teeth, he tore the envelope open and cursed when he read the notice.

Val was suing for custody.

The sounds of the chatter and din in the restaurant faded away around him, and all he heard was the crinkle of paper as his fist closed around the notice. She'd threatened to sue for custody, but he hadn't quite believed her. He'd thought maybe she was bluffing just to get him to relent and let her take Olive back to Southern California for some acting career his little girl didn't even want.

Everything in him tensed, and anger coiled in his gut, quickly coursing through his veins until he was practically vibrating with the toxic emotion.

"Boss?" Rhys asked. "You all right?"

"No." Clay turned hard eyes on his assistant. "I have to go take care of something. Can you manage here without me for the rest of the afternoon?"

"Sure. Not a problem. What's wrong?"

Clay carefully folded the crumbled notice and put it back into the envelope. Then he answered with one word. "Val."

CLAY WALKED INTO THE OFFICE OF LORNA WHITE AND GLANCED around at the cozy atmosphere. Overstuffed, cream-colored chairs filled the space near the front window. A matching loveseat sat in front of the crackling fireplace.

"Clay, hello," Paige, Lorna's daughter, said as she stood and walked over to him. "Mom was wondering when you'd finally come visit us."

"She was expecting me?" he asked, wondering if Yvette had said something to her.

Paige brushed a lock of her black hair out of her eyes and shrugged one shoulder. "She's met Val. No one expected you to get out of the marriage without some sort of battle."

He let out a humorless laugh. "Yeah, well, I got out of the marriage. But now we have custody issues."

"Oh, Clay, I'm sorry to hear it," she said, concern and sympathy radiating in her tone.

"Thanks," he said. "Is Lorna free?"

She held up one finger. "Give me just a minute."

As Paige disappeared into her mother's office, Clay took a seat in one of the overstuffed chairs. The office was unlike anything he'd expect from a lawyer's office. There wasn't anything sterile about the place, and if he didn't know better, he'd think Lorna White was an interior decorator or event planner. The atmosphere was just too comfortable.

"Mr. Garrison." Lorna strode out of her office and took a seat in the chair next to him. "I can't say it's good to see you. Not under these circumstances, anyway."

Clay offered his hand, and she clasped it in both of hers. "I have to admit, I would be happier if this was a just a social call, Lorna." He handed her the subpoena for the custody hearing. "She's suing for full custody."

Lorna grimaced. "Playing hardball, is she?"

"It's the only way she knows how to play."

She nodded her understanding. "How's that pretty little girl of yours doing with all of this?"

He shook his head. "She doesn't know yet. But Val has been trying to force her into acting. Olive isn't into it, but she's been going along to please her mother."

"Acting? Wow. That's a lot for an eight-year-old. How do you feel about it?"

Clay shook his head. "To be honest, Lorna, I hate it. And I fear Val thinks that if she can book work for Olive that it will somehow further her own career."

"Do you have any evidence of that?"

"No." Clay sighed. "Only a couple of things Olive told me about her mother trying to book them jobs together."

"Okay." She flipped open a notebook and jotted down a couple of notes. "I assume you're here for representation?"

"Yes, but…" Clay grimaced.

"What is it, Clay?" Lorna studied him, her head tilted to the side.

He blew out a breath. "I don't have a lot of cash on hand. Between shuffling Olive back and forth from here to Los Angeles and supporting Val, things are a little tight."

She waved a hand. "Let's not worry about that now. It's more important that we keep your girl here in Keating Hollow."

"But, I don't know I'm going to pay—"

"We'll work something out, Clay. Please, don't worry about it."

Clay rolled his shoulders easing some of his tension. "Okay. I'll make payments, as much as I can. Do you need a retainer?"

She shook her head and stood. "Let's go into my office. We can go over everything I need to know."

"All right." As Clay rose and followed Lorna into an office that had the same vibe as her reception area, he realized her brilliance. He'd walked in the office tense and antsy with irritation. But just sitting in her waiting room and talking informally had already eased some of his tension. For him, that was exactly what he needed. Otherwise he'd lose his mind.

In Lorna's office, Clay sat in a comfortable armchair in front of her desk. She poured them both a cup of coffee and sat across from him, pen in hand. "Okay, tell me everything about Val, the good, the bad, the ugly. And don't hold back."

Clay sucked in a deep breath. "Okay, but remember… you asked for it."

CHAPTER 16

*a*bby sat at the dining room table, working through her emails. A lot of product requests for the holidays had come in over the last few days, which meant she was going to have to get it together and get back to work. Ever since her failure to complete the potion for her dad, she'd been putting off making any new inventory. She just didn't have it in her to use her magic, even if she knew it was working well enough for her product line.

The lead of the mechanical pencil scratched against the notebook paper as she logged the ingredients she'd need to restock. She was so engrossed in her work that it took her a moment to realize someone was laying into a horn out front of their house.

She got up and checked on her dad, finding him in the kitchen indulging in the brownies she'd made the night before. *Finally,* she thought. He'd barely eaten over the last few days, and while a brownie was hardly the height of nutrition, the calories were very welcome.

"Hey," she said. "You expecting someone?"

"Nope," he said and took a sip of his coffee. "None of my friends drive a party golf cart."

"What? How do you know there's a party cart out there?" she asked, laughing.

"I can tell by that sad horn." He gave her a bob of his head. "Go on. Wanda's waiting."

Abby shook her head. How he knew Wanda was waiting, she had no idea. Sometimes he just had a strange sixth sense about things. She walked over and gave him a kiss on the cheek. "You're something else, you know that?"

"That's what the ladies tell me."

Abby groaned and headed out to the front of their house. Sure enough, Wanda was sitting in her party cart, Bruno Mars blaring from the speakers. Her freshly dyed red hair bounced around her smiling face as she danced in her seat, arms raised in the air.

"Well, hello there," Abby said, grinning at her. "What's going on?"

"I came to kidnap you. Hop in." She patted the seat next to her.

Abby glanced back at her house, chewing on her bottom lip. Her dad was having a good day.

"Come on. Live a little, Townsend. You've been home for over a week and no one has seen you. Well, no one but Clay." She pumped her eyebrows. "I bet that was *interesting*."

"What makes you think I've seen Clay?"

"Please." She laughed, the sound so infectious it made Abby smile. "Everyone at the brewery is talking about you two being holed-up in the brew shed. Don't even try to deny it."

"I'm not," Abby said as she rounded the cart and climbed in. "I just wanted to know who was talking about me." She shrugged. "He was helping me out."

"Is that what we're calling it these days?" She winked, making it clear she was just teasing.

Abby considered explaining what exactly they'd been working on, but dismissed the idea. She didn't need everyone's advice on fixing her magic, and that's exactly what she would get if the town found out she was trying to practice again. "If by 'it' you mean just friends, then sure."

Wanda shook her head, her expression amused. "Girl, nothing about you and Clay was ever 'just friends.' But if that's the call you want to make, I'm with you."

"You know, you're right about that. But this time, Wanda, it's true. We're just friends, or at least we're friendly. We have a lot of history to unpack before we're besties."

"I hear that." Wanda put the cart in gear and turned around. "You never did call me for that midnight run down by the lake. You up for it this weekend?"

The sun was shining down on them, warming not only Abby's skin but also her heart. And with her dad doing okay, Abby couldn't resist. "Yes. I'll bring the Irish cocoa."

"Now you're talkin' my language." Wanda waved at the beverage holder. "There's liquid courage in that water bottle if you need it."

"Liquid courage? For what?" Abby asked.

"I found out who owns that white Mini Cooper you took out your first day in town." Wanda paused at the end of the driveway then took a left turn, away from town. There were only a couple of houses out that way, including one Abby knew just as well as her own home.

"Wanda?" Abby asked, her heart racing. "Please tell me we aren't going where I think we're going."

"Sorry. No can do." The song shifted, and Abba started pouring out of the speakers. "Turns out that Mini Cooper belongs to none other than Mary Pelsh."

Abby closed her eyes and took deep breaths, trying to settle herself. She hadn't seen Charlotte's mom since the funeral, though Hanna told her every chance she got that Charlotte's parents really wanted to see Abby. And now she was going to make her grand debut by confessing to smashing in the rear of their brand new car.

"Just perfect," she muttered. Of course it belonged to Mary. The way the universe had been working against her, that new development made perfect sense. She turned to Wanda. "Did we have to go right this minute?"

"No, but you know how gossip spreads through this town. She's bound to find out it was you sooner rather than later, and I figured this isn't something you want to let fester." She pointed at the water bottle. "Drink. You need it."

Abby eyed the bottle and raised a curious eyebrow. "What it is?"

"Booze! Don't ask stupid questions. Just do what you have to do."

"Right," Abby said and grabbed the booze bottle. Then before she could think too hard about it, she twisted off the cap, and took a large swig. The Crown and Coke hit the back of her throat, and she winced as she forced it down. Abby wasn't big on drinking hard alcohol, but she had to hand it to Wanda; if ever there was a time for it, this was it.

Wanda winked at her and steered the cart down the long winding driveway that led to the Pelsh's property. Abby put the bottle back in the cup holder, thinking better of showing up sauced. That wasn't how she wanted to speak to them for the first time in years. She had to get ahold of herself.

"Ready?" Wanda asked, pulling to a stop in front of their modest one story home.

"No." But Abby climbed out of the cart anyway. Now that she was here, the desire to see Mary was overwhelming.

Emotion welled in her chest, and suddenly it was a little harder to breathe. Still, her feet seemed to move on their own up the flower-lined walkway until she was standing at their front door.

Wanda was right behind her, and before Abby could change her mind, Wanda pressed the doorbell. Abby heard it ring inside the house, followed by the sharp bark of a dog.

The door swung open and Mary Pelsh appeared wearing leggings, a long tunic, and chic, black, knee-high boots. Shock rolled over her face as her dark eyes widened and her mouth dropped open. Then she gasped as she stepped onto the porch and wrapped Abby in her arms.

"Abigail," she said with a relieved sigh. "Hanna told me you were in town. I was so hoping you'd come by and see us."

"I'm sorry," Abby blurted and squeezed the woman who'd been like a second mother to her. "I'm so, so sorry."

Mary pulled back slightly, searching Abby's face. "Whatever do you have to be sorry about?"

Abby shook her head, unable to speak as the tears rolled down her cheeks.

"Oh, sweetie. Come in. I'll get you a tissue and something to drink." Mary glanced over Abby's shoulder and nodded at Wanda. "You, too. Let's go sit and chat a bit."

Mary kept her arm entwined with Abby's as she guided her into the bright, sunny kitchen. "Have a seat," she said, waving at the breakfast table. "I'll get us some tea."

"Thanks, Mary," Wanda said and sat next to Abby near the bay window that looked out on the redwood forest.

Mary grabbed a sparkly wand, pointed it at the kettle on the stove, and said, "Prepare the tea." The cabinet door just to the left of the stove opened, and a container of loose leaf tea flew out. The kettle floated to the sink where the faucet turned on by itself and filled the pot.

Abby couldn't help but smile as she watched the spectacle. Mary was an air witch and extremely gifted at telekinesis. Only it was more than just moving objects with her mind. It was almost as if she communicated with the air around her, willing it to choreograph the dance required to make everything come together to produce the perfect cup of tea.

"How about a pastry or two?" Without waiting for an answer, Mary pointed her wand at a plate of Danishes and sent them to the table. Napkins, plates, and spoons followed, landing gently in front of both Wanda and Abby.

"Your skills have really improved, Mrs. P," Abby said. "I can still remember the time you made cupcakes for Charlotte's birthday." She turned to Wanda. "But when she sent them to the table, they flew through the air spinning around and around and most of them ended up splattered on the table." Abby laughed, still remembering the horrified look on Charlotte's face. "But that was nothing compared to when one hit Andrew Baker right in his… um…" Abby pointed to her lap. "The kids started calling him cupcake balls."

"Oh, that was horrible. Charlotte had a crush on him, too," Mary added.

Abby nodded. "She sure did. And when they finally started dating in high school, she always affectionately called him cupcake."

"So that's where that nickname came from." Wanda laughed. "You know he works at the police station now, and the other officers call him that. I just figured it was a rookie-hazing kind of thing."

Abby shook her head. "Nope."

"Thank goodness he's always been a good-natured guy, or that could've scarred him for life," Mary said with a shudder. "After that, I stopped showing off if the kids had friends over. I didn't want another cupcake balls incident."

"You've got nothing to worry about now Mrs. P. Charlotte would be proud," Abby said and was surprised to find that, for once, talking about Charlotte didn't make her want to vomit. In fact, it was kind of nice to remember her as she was before she got sick.

"Thanks. I like to think so." Mary took a seat next to Abby and pushed the Danishes in her direction. "Eat. You need something to soak up the alcohol in your system."

"I..." Abby narrowed her eyes at Mary. "How did you know I'd had a drink? It was just one sip."

"Air witch, remember?" She tapped her temple. "I just know things."

Wanda snorted. "More like she can smell it."

"That too." Mary took a cheese Danish and tore off a piece before adding, "I have an extremely sensitive nose. If it's in the air, I'm aware of it."

Of course. Abby should've remembered that. Mrs. P could scent out just about anything—boys, booze, bullshit. She'd kept them on their toes, for sure. Abby grabbed a Danish of her own and nibbled on a small piece until the tea floated through the air and landed softly right in front of her. She picked up the cup and took a sip of the blueberry and sage blend. "It's delicious."

"It's a favorite of mine." Mary took her own sip and eyed Abby. "Now, Abigail, I think it's time you told me exactly why you've stayed away for so long. You know we wanted to see you."

Abby swallowed the rest of her pastry, her mouth suddenly dry, and she shook her head. "I just... couldn't. Not after what happened."

Mary's hand closed over Abby's. "And what is it you think happened?"

"I..." Abby looked to Wanda as if she had the answer, but

Wanda hadn't been there. She didn't know what Abby knew. Finally, she turned and looked Mary in the eyes. "It's my fault Charlotte died. I gave her an energy potion that masked her symptoms, and instead of asking for help, she tried to go to that stupid dance instead."

Tears filled Mary's eyes as she squeezed Abby's hand harder. "You are not the reason Charlotte isn't with us, Abby. You were only trying to help. No one blames you."

"I do." Abby's voice was hollow, void of emotion. She had to get through this and finally say what she'd been holding in for so many years. "If it wasn't for me, she would've been too weak to leave the house. You or your husband would've noticed and taken her to the healer, a *real* healer who knew what to do for her. Instead, because of me, she was feeling good that night. Good enough to put on that prom dress and act like everything was just fine. But it wasn't. She was dying, and we were dancing, celebrating that we had our whole lives in front of us. If I'd known, I never would've... well, there are lots of things I'd do differently."

Mary sat in silence, her eyes closed, shaking her head.

"I'm so, so sorry," Abby said again and got up from the table. "I should go now. I never wanted to add to your pain. It's why—"

"Abby!" Mary grabbed her hand and held on tightly. "There's something you don't know. Please have a seat."

Abby froze, unsure of how to proceed. She'd been so certain the Pelshes would hate her after they found out she'd given Charlotte a potion when they'd specifically asked her not to. They'd asked her to let their healers deal with Charlotte's illness. But Charlotte had told Abby it was just an infection. What could possible go wrong? The medication they'd had her on would clear it right up. What harm would a little energy potion be?

Mary's sad eyes searched Abby's. Then she averted her gaze and stared at the pastry in front of her. "Charlotte was sick for a long time."

"What?" Abby and Wanda asked at the same time.

"She had an autoimmune disease that caused her to have a weakened immune system."

Abby blinked. "She had an autoimmune disease? But how... I mean, why did she never tell us that?"

"She didn't want anyone to treat her any differently," Mary said with a sigh. "You remember how she'd be out sick a couple days every few months?"

"But she wasn't really sick. She told us... oh." Abby shook her head. How could she be so stupid? Charlotte had told them her mom liked to have spontaneous mother-daughter days where they'd head off to the beach or go out of town on long weekends. Abby had been so jealous, never questioning it might not be the truth.

"Technically, she wasn't usually sick. We were off getting her treatments with a specialist in Salem. The disease she had is rare and only shows up in one percent of female witches. A healer back east was treating her. But eventually, the treatments stopped working."

They stopped working. The words rang in Abby's mind. Her friend had been very sick, and she'd known nothing about it. "What did you do?"

Mary pressed her lips together into a thin line, clearly struggling through this conversation. "We were trying some experimental treatments with a healer who was studying at Humboldt State. It was all trials. Most didn't pan out, but one was promising and seemed to be helping. Then she got that lung infection. By then, she'd been battling her disease for ten years, Abby. She was fed up and just wanted to keep living her life. I'm not surprised she asked you for the energy potion. She was tired of missing out on life."

"I appreciate that, Mrs. P. But I still don't see how I'm not at fault. If I hadn't—"

"She was dying, Abby. When she got the lung infection, the new treatment ceased to be effective. There was nothing out there to save her," Mary said gently. "Don't you see? Charlotte died living. It was her wish. She didn't want to be wasting away in a bed. She wanted to live life to the fullest, and you helped her do that."

Abby stood abruptly, unable to accept what her friend's mom was saying. "I know you're trying to let me off the hook here, and I appreciate the effort, but I can't ignore the fact that my potion caused her early demise." Tears filled her eyes again, and she did nothing to stop them from spilling down her cheeks. "That's something I'll have to live with the rest of my life, knowing that you didn't get to say goodbye, that she should've still had more time, that I went against your wishes. I was arrogant and thought I knew better. That arrogance cost me my best friend. So please, don't try to make me feel better."

Silence hung in the kitchen. Abby started to feel like a trapped animal, like the walls were closing in on her. She had to get out of there. Now. She turned to go, but Mary stood just as abruptly and wrapped her arms around Abby, clutching her so tightly Abby's ribs started to ache.

"It's not your fault. It's not your fault," Mary said over and over and over again. "Someday I hope you learn to stop blaming yourself because it's not your fault. It never was and never could be."

Abby hung on to Mary, letting herself be comforted in her embrace, but still knowing the truth. Her actions had taken her best friend from the earth too soon. The pain that knowledge brought her wasn't likely to fade.

"Promise me something?" Mary asked.

"Anything," Abby said, knowing she owed Mary whatever she asked for.

"Go see someone. Talk to someone about this."

Abby stiffened. "I don't—"

"Please, Abby." Mary let her go and scooted around the counter. She reached in a drawer and produced a business card. "Talk to Doctor Kass. She really helped me get through the pain after we lost Charlotte."

"I did talk to someone in New Orleans." Abby ran her hands down her tear-stained face. "It didn't... Well let's just say it made things worse."

"Oh, honey." Mary grabbed her hands again. "I'm so sorry that didn't work out. But Doctor Kass was a lifesaver. Nothing but a comfort to me. At least try? Try for Charlotte? She wouldn't want you to be in such pain after all these years."

How could Abby say no to her? She couldn't. Nodding, she said, "I'll call."

"Good, that's good," Mary said, sounding relieved. "You won't regret it."

Abby was one hundred percent certain she would, but she gave Mary a weak smile anyway and said, 'We should probably go." But when she glanced around, she noted Wanda had disappeared. She frowned. "Where's Wanda?"

Mary glanced around the kitchen. "Maybe she just wanted to give us a minute."

That was probable. Abby started to walk toward the front door, but then she remembered the reason she'd come in the first place. "Um, Mrs. P?"

"Yes?" She waved her sparkling wand, sending the tea and pastries back to the kitchen counter.

"Do you own a white Mini Cooper?"

"Yes, why?"

"Did your niece borrow it to take it for a spin a week or so ago?" Abby grimaced. "And did it come back with the back end smashed in?"

Mary eyed her with suspicion. "Borrow isn't the word I'd use, but yes, she drove my car. How do you know about that? Candy said it was a hit and run."

Abby sighed. "I guess you could call it that. I'm the one who hit your car."

"Abby." Mary dragged her name out as she shook her head.

"But I'm not the one who ran. You can even check with Pauly Putzner. He was there to take my statement, but before he could get all the information, your niece—Candy—took off. I'm so sorry. It was just an accident. I've already informed my insurance company. They just need the police report and an estimate."

"She took off?" Mary's eyes narrowed in irritation. "Why?"

"I think she was afraid she might get in trouble. I don't know. But because she fled, I had no idea who to get in touch with. Wanda was the one who realized the car belonged to you, so I came to make things right."

Her expression softened. "Thanks, Abby. Just leave your insurance information and I'll pass it along to my agent. And I really appreciate you coming by today." She held her arms out, inviting another hug. Unable to resist, Abby stepped into her embrace.

They held each other for a long moment, and then Abby stepped back and brushed the fresh tears from her eyes. Once she'd relayed her insurance information, she waved and walked outside, finding Wanda lounging in her golf cart.

"What are you doing out here?" Abby asked.

"Just soaking up some sun. I thought you two could use a moment." She held up a chocolate stout beer bottle. "Also I was thirsty for something a little stronger than tea."

146

Abby laughed as she took her spot in the cart.

"Abby, wait!" Mary called, running out the door with a medium-sized gift box in her hand. "I've been saving this for you." She handed it over. "It's some of Charlotte's mementos I thought you'd like to have one day."

Abby clutched the box, both curious and a little frightened to see what was inside. But the truth was she missed her friend. And after spending ten years trying to not think about her, she'd really enjoyed reminiscing with Mary. The cupcake story had helped lift a little bit of weight off her heart, and if the contents of the box could do the same thing, Abby thought she might be ready to take another walk down memory lane. "Thanks, Mrs. P. I appreciate it."

She waved a dismissive hand. "It's no big deal. Don't be a stranger, Abby, you hear?"

"I won't," Abby promised. And this time she meant it.

CHAPTER 17

After Clay's visit to the lawyer's office, he stopped in at his mother's house to check on Olive. His little girl was as feisty and rambunctious as ever while she played in the tree house with the boy next door. He watched from his mother's kitchen window as Olive and her playmate pretended the treehouse was a fort they were defending with arrows from the evil ghost army from beyond the veil.

He chuckled, his heart full.

"She loves it here," his mom said, standing next to him. She wore an apron over her dusty jeans and T-shirt and had dirt embedded under her fingernails, a sure sign she'd been fussing with her garden. "I never saw her like this when you lived in L.A."

Clay nodded. "You're right. But then she never had the freedom down there that she does here, either. The city is a very different place to grow up."

"I'm not sure it was the city so much as perhaps her mother's ambition."

He hated that his mother was right. Val had always wanted

Olive to be the prim and proper little girl, perfectly behaved, perfectly coiffed as if she were a porcelain doll. It wasn't that Val subscribed to the theory that children should be seen but not heard, she just acted as if Olive's every move reflected upon Val and her ability to land her next job.

Clay cursed himself for ever agreeing to let Val take her to any auditions in the first place. Val had quickly learned that Olive had a face for television. The casting directors loved her —or they did until Olive got impatient and started getting on their nerves with her excessive chatter brought on by pure boredom.

"You have a point," Clay said.

"She doesn't like acting, you know that right?"

Clay nodded. "Yes. She doesn't come out and say it, but it's pretty obvious."

His mom raised her eyebrows. "Really? She's told me plenty of times."

He turned to her. "When?"

"All the time. Pretty much every time she comes back from seeing her mom. She doesn't talk about it with you?"

"No." He shoved his hands in his front pockets and hunched his shoulders. "She's protecting Val."

His mother shook her head, and her freshly dyed, honey-kissed curls bobbed around her face "Well, I'm not gonna protect her. You know I don't like criticizing Olive's mother—"

"Really?" Clay asked, chuckling. "Since when?"

She placed her hands on her hips. "Hey, I held my tongue while you two were still married."

"True. You did. And I appreciated it, though you haven't exactly spared me your feelings over the last year and a half."

Marina Garrison stared Clay in the eyes and said, "Son, I respect you and your decisions. And I also love you and Olive. But I can't and won't stand by while her mother does her best to destroy that little girl's spirit. And that's what she does every time she takes her to L.A. Did you know she didn't talk to anyone for two days after she came home this last time?"

"She spoke to me," he said, frowning.

"Yeah. Just you. But not me. Not Randy." She waved a hand indicating the boy outside. "And she barely spoke to anyone at school. Her teacher said it was like her lights were off then all of a sudden someone flipped a switch."

"I knew she was upset after the way Val left, but I didn't realize it was that bad. Why didn't you tell me?"

"I was going to, but then she snapped out of it and you were already angry enough at Val. But now that she's suing for custody, I thought you needed to know."

Clay nodded. "Yeah. Thanks."

"I'm sorry, honey."

He glanced over at her. "You've got nothing to be sorry for, Mom."

~

CLAY WAS STILL FUMING WHEN HE WALKED INTO THE BREWERY. Valerie was a piece of work. Didn't she care at all about what she was doing to their daughter? He shook his head. It was obvious she didn't. Not when she was set on forcing her to do something she didn't want to do.

Instead of checking in with Rhys and the rest of the staff, he headed straight for his office. He was in no mood to talk to anyone. He sat at his desk and stared blankly at the recipe he'd been working on, but it was no use. His frustration had turned to agitation, and he was restless.

He stood, grabbed the baseball off his desk, and tossed it from hand to hand as he paced his office. The idea that Val would try for full custody was ludicrous. Surely the fact that she'd abandoned them would count against her in the court proceedings. He'd never understood how Abby's mother could've left her daughters. And he certainly didn't understand how Val had left Olive either.

With Abby on his mind, he glanced out the office window toward the old brew shed. And that's when he saw her. She was standing in front of the window, her head bowed as she focused on her work. Something inside Clay shifted as he watched her. He was calmer, as if her presence settled him. At just that moment, Abby glanced up and their eyes met. Her lips curved into a whisper of a smile, sending an unexpected jolt of joy straight to his heart. Without another thought, he placed the baseball on his desk and headed out to the shed.

"Hey there." Abby grinned at him the moment he walked through the door. "It's been a few days, hasn't it?"

"Only because you've been slacking," he said, smiling lazily at her.

"Slacking?" She laughed, her eyes sparkling.

He grinned at her like a fool, all too aware he was seeing a freer, happier Abigail than the one who'd rolled into town over a week ago. The glimpse he was getting of this Abby was the one he'd known back in high school, the one he'd fallen in love with.

"How do you know I've been slacking? Been keeping an eye out for me, Garrison?"

"So what if I have?" he said, moving to stand closer to her, unable to avoid her magnetic pull. He'd never been able to. There was no reason to believe he'd be immune now. Not when she was so obviously the same person, only richer, more layered, more complicated.

She placed her hands on his chest and tilted her head to look him in the eyes. "I think you know where to find me if you're looking for me."

His breath caught as he gazed at her lovely face, the openness there shining back at him, the trust, the goodness. She was everything Val wasn't, and it took his breath away.

"You know, at home treating the orchard and making sure Dad has a decent lunch to eat. Who ever thought I'd turn into the domestic goddess of the family?"

He chuckled and took a step back. "Not me. But speaking of your family, are your sisters coming around to help out?"

"Sure. Faith swings by most days. But Yvette is busy at her store, and Noel has Daisy. It just so happens I'm the one who's living there. So Faith mostly entertains Dad and keeps him in good spirits while I make sure everything is running smoothly. It's not a burden."

"I wouldn't dream of thinking it was, not for you, anyway. Family always was your priority," he said.

"Was... until I left." She turned and focused on an open box on her work station.

It was then he realized she hadn't been working at all. Or at least hadn't started working. The only thing on the stainless steel counter was the box and two photographs. He peered at them, recognizing the photos of her and Charlotte at the beach, photos he'd taken. "Whoa," he said softly. "I haven't seen those since we got them developed. Where'd you get those?"

"Charlotte's mom. I went to see Mrs. P today."

Sympathy mixed with surprise flashed over his face as his eyes widened. "Looks like it went well enough. You doing okay?"

"Yeah," Abby said softly. "Okay enough. It was hard but also good. We reminisced a bit. Talking about her was easier than I expected."

Clay's heart swelled with emotion. He hadn't seen Abby this peaceful since before Charlotte died. He wanted to live in the moment for forever. He'd missed *this* Abby. "She wouldn't have wanted you to shut her away in your memories. You know that right?"

"I do." She gazed up at him, her eyes glassy from the tears she was holding back. "It just usually hurts way too much."

"And now?" He couldn't resist reaching up and tucking a strand of her blond hair behind her ear.

She blinked and her eyes cleared. "It still hurts, but talking about her seems to be healing, too. Mrs. P wants me to talk to a therapist."

He wished she'd gone to see one ten years ago. When she'd broken up with him and made it clear she was leaving town, he'd asked her to talk to a professional before making such a huge life change, but she'd bolted. "If you find the right one, they can usually help. What did you say?"

She let out a choked laugh. "I told her about the quack I saw down in New Orleans who only made me feel worse about everything."

His eyebrows shot up his forehead. "You did talk to someone? I thought... well, I guess I thought you were against the idea."

She pressed a hand to his chest right over his heart. "You asked me to right after we lost Charlotte, so when I got to New Orleans, I did."

Clay brought his hand up and covered hers, holding her hand there. "I'm sorry it didn't go well."

"Me too. Mrs. P says sometimes you have to keep trying them out until you find the right fit."

"That's usually true. I did before I found Doctor Bell."

"You saw a therapist?" Her voice was high and disbelieving.

He gave her a wry smile. "Well, sure. I was suffering from some serious abandonment issues. When Val left, I started to really take it personally, you know? First you, then her. It starts to really mess with a guy's head." Abby winced and tried to pull back, but Clay kept his hand clasped over hers, keeping her in place and added, "Don't run again, Abs. Not now. We still have business to settle."

"Clay, I—"

"You don't have to say anything, Abby. That's not why I brought this up. I only wanted you to know that sometimes, a lot of the time, speaking to the right professional can really help you sort out the crap that's tearing you up inside. I just want you to be at peace with the past."

She studied him then shifted her gaze to their hands still interlocked over his heart. "Are you?"

He sucked in a shuddering breath, caught a little off-guard by her question. "Are you sure you want to know that answer to that?"

"Yes." Her answer was immediate and full of conviction.

"Okay, but remember, you wanted to know."

Abby nodded. "More than you can possibly imagine."

Clay was certain she was going to regret asking. Certainly, he was going to regret answering, but he couldn't lie. Not when everything inside of him was screaming for him to kiss her. "Feel that flutter of my heart beneath your hand?"

She frowned. "Yeah."

"That has everything to do with you. With your presence. With this quiet friendship we've restarted. With the fact that ever since you walked back into this town, I haven't been able to get you out of my head."

"You haven't?" she asked, giving him a hint of a smile.

"No. Not even for a minute. So the answer is definitely no. I have not made peace with my past. Not all of it. Most of it, sure. But when it comes to you, Abigail Townsend, my past with you will always haunt me. I've wanted you since I was thirteen years old, and ten years of being apart has done nothing to change that fact. I *want* you in my life, Abby. But that hasn't been my choice for a decade. So I did the only thing I could do—"

"Marry someone else," she said. Her attempt at a smile was more of wince.

He let out a humorless chuckle and shook his head. "No, I learned to deal with the fact you weren't coming back to me, to us. So while I can accept what has happened, even move on from it and lead a normal existence, it's not what I wanted. I suspect it will never be what I want, but it isn't my call to make. It's yours and always has been."

Abby made a light strangled noise in the back of her throat as she pressed her palm harder to Clay's chest. "I'm so sorry, Clay," she said again. "So, so sorry. I never wanted to hurt you."

"I know, Abs. It's okay." He brought one hand up and caressed her cheek.

Her body careened toward his as she leaned into him, her eyes closed. Everything about her took his breath away. He knew it was a bad idea to let himself fall for her all over again when she had a life she'd eventually go back to in New Orleans. But there was no stopping what was happening between them. When it came to Abigail Townsend, Clay didn't know how to walk away.

With his heart in his throat, he closed the distance between them and pressed his lips to hers.

CHAPTER 18

*A*bby's insides melted. Warmth and joy and desire mixed together, filling her up as she slid one hand into Clay's thick hair and pressed the other one to his chest. His lips moved softly over hers, gentle, yet firm, and quickly turned slightly demanding when his arms tightened around her. He bowed her back, opening his mouth to deepen the kiss.

The world stopped and faded away. All she knew was Clay Garrison and the way she felt in his arms—wanted, loved, desired.

"Abby?" A man's angry voice filled the shed. "What are you doing?"

She froze, recognizing Logan's outraged tone immediately.

Clay straightened, bringing Abby with him, then turned around, keeping one arm around her waist. He glanced over at her. "You know this person?"

Abby nodded and took a step forward. "Logan, what are you doing here?"

"Looking for my girlfriend. Imagine my shock to find her

kissing someone else. Is this the real reason you aren't coming home?"

"What?" She stared at him, her mouth slightly open as she tried to process what he'd said. *Girlfriend?* Had he conveniently forgotten her email and their phone call last week?

Clay stiffened beside her and cleared his throat. "I thought you said you broke up."

"We did!" Abby said, alarmed by the accusation in Clay's tone. "I ended it last week. Twice." She turned her attention back to Logan. "Did you think you could just show up here and pretend that conversation never happened?"

"No, of course not," Logan said reasonably, taking Abby's hand in his. "But you can't just break up with someone over the phone after two years of living together. Abby, we have something special, and I won't let you throw it away."

Abby stared down at their connection, his touch simultaneously familiar and foreign. She glanced at Clay.

He raised his eyebrows. "You lived together?"

"What? Goddess no." She snatched her hand away from Logan, anger finally catching up to her shock at seeing him in Keating Hollow. She met Logan's patronizing gaze. "We never lived together. Why are you revising history? And why are you here?"

"Come on, Abby. We might as well have been living together. And I know you're just stressed. We can't break up while you're dealing with your dad. You're being irrational."

Clay let out a snort of laughter and mumbled, "That isn't going to go over well."

"No, it isn't," Abby said, placing her hands on her hips. "I don't know who you think you are, or why you're here in my work shed, but I can assure you, you aren't welcome, Logan. How did you even get back here?"

"Abby, baby, come on. Let's go for a walk and talk this out."

"No. And don't call me baby." Abby crossed her arms over her chest and glared at him. "Who let you back here?"

Logan waved a hand at the side entrance to the pub. "The guy running the place said you were probably working back here. I figured I'd surprise you."

Abby placed her hand on his chest and pushed him back out of the shed. "Consider me surprised. Now move."

Logan dug his heels in and used the shed door to brace himself. "Abby—"

"Listen, pal," Clay said calmly. "It's pretty obvious Abby isn't all that happy to see you. I suggest you do what she says before I call the police and have you removed from the premises."

Logan narrowed his eyes at Clay. "Back off, buddy. Abby is *my* girlfriend."

"No, I'm not!" Abby yelled at the top of her lungs. Then she just stared at Logan, taking in his disapproving expression and his clenched fists. Finally, she shook her head in exasperation and brushed past him, stalking into the pub. She knew without glancing back that he'd followed her, and she just kept right on going through the front doors and down the wooden steps until she was in the parking lot. "Which is your rental car?"

"The black BMW," Logan said from behind her.

"Of course it is," she said dryly and walked over to the nicest car in the lot. When she turned around, she spotted Clay standing on the porch, leaning against the railing, watching her. She gave him a slight nod, a silent *thank you* for watching over her but giving her the space she needed to handle the situation herself. Turning her attention to Logan, she asked, "Why did you come here?"

He took a step forward, but Abby held her hand up, stopping him. He sighed. "To talk you out of this hasty breakup. We're good together, Abigail. You don't want to ruin a good thing over some small-town bartender."

"You mean Clay?" She laughed at his assumption, but inside she just wanted to cry or scream again. Hadn't Logan heard anything she'd said to him? "First of all, he isn't a bartender. He's a master brewer, and he runs my dad's business. Second, our breakup has nothing to do with him. It has to do with you. I'm tired of you not listening to me, Logan. Everything is always about you and what you need. Right now, I have to take care of me and my family. And I can't do that while I'm worrying about you trying to get me back to New Orleans."

He glanced at Clay and scowled.

"Oh my goddess!" Abby threw her hands up. "Go home, Logan. This is the last time I'm saying this: We. Are. Done. I'm no longer your girlfriend. I'm sorry you came all this way, but you should've called first."

"Abby..."

She shook her head and started to walk away.

Logan reached out and grabbed her arm, stopping her.

Abby froze and stared at his hand gripping her. "Let go," she said through clenched teeth.

"Not until you talk to me," Logan said stubbornly.

"You better let the lady go," Clay said, striding up to them. "The sheriff's on his way, and if he sees you handling Abby like that, there's going to be hell to pay."

Abby yanked her arm out of Logan's grip and took a step toward him, invading his personal space. "If you ever touch me again, I'll get a restraining order. Got it?"

He held his hands up in the air. "Fine. Got it. No need to be so dramatic. I just wanted—"

"I don't care what you wanted. Get in your car and go. I don't know how many more ways to say this." Abby shook her head. "I don't want to be your girlfriend anymore. And if you don't leave me alone, you're gonna have bigger problems than the sheriff." She glanced down at his crotch. "You don't want me to curse your manbits, do you?"

Logan's face turned pale. "You wouldn't."

"Try me."

"Damn, Abby. I thought you were more mature than that. Grow up, will you?"

"You first."

Grumbling to himself, he slid back into his flashy BMW. After rolling his window down, he leaned out and said, "You're going to regret this."

"I seriously doubt it."

Logan slammed the car into gear and peeled out of the parking lot, leaving rubber behind on the asphalt.

Abby stood there fuming as she watched the car fly down Main Street. She could barely wrap her head around the fact that her ex had just shown up and dismissed everything she'd said to him over the phone as if it hadn't happened. Then he'd treated her like she was the crazy one. She sucked in a deep breath and blew it out.

"You doing okay?" Clay softly asked from behind her.

She closed her eyes, once again wishing the ground would just open up and swallow her whole. How had she ever been involved with a man who was so egotistical, so out of touch with reality, that he'd flown two thousand miles across the country thinking she'd just dismiss his selfish behavior and forget she wanted to breakup?

Clay placed his hand on the small of her back. "Abby?"

"I'm all right," she said with a sigh. "Did that really just happen?"

"Afraid so, but I'm impressed at your ability to scare him off. Curse his manbits, huh? Did you learn a few new tricks over the years, or were you just bluffing?"

Abby laughed. "Obviously I was bluffing, but did you see the look on his face?"

"That's the Abby I remember." Clay grinned and held his hand out to her.

She slipped her hand into his and smiled up at him. "Did you really call the sheriff?"

"No, but I was thinking about it. That guy seemed a little out of touch with reality."

"A little?" Abby rolled her eyes. "That's a bit of an understatement. You know what I don't understand?"

"What's that?"

"How could I have been in a relationship with him for two years and not seen what an ass he could be?"

Clay gave her a sad smile and shook his head. "I've asked myself a similar question about Val all too many times, Abby. I think some people are just good at showing us who they think we want them to be, but eventually the cracks form and there's no denying their true colors. All we can do is hope they show them before it's too late."

"Two years is a long time. I think I was deliberately trying *not* to see his true nature."

"You're one of the lucky ones. Try seven and then get back to me," he said, sadness reflecting back at her in his dark eyes.

Abby placed her hand on his chest over his heart, wishing with everything she had that she could undo the pain he'd suffered. She didn't exactly blame herself. They'd still been kids when she'd left Keating Hollow. If she'd never run off, who was to say they'd have stayed together and still been a couple a decade later? But she *did* know she'd loved him, and that love was still buried deep inside her. Knowing he'd been through a rough marriage that had ended in divorce made her heart ache for him.

A light autumn breeze kicked up and blew a piece of Abby's

hair into her eyes. Clay reached up and brushed it back, making gooseflesh pop up over her skin. She shivered slightly, wanting to be back in his embrace as she had been before Logan had so rudely interrupted them.

Their eyes met, and Clay smiled down at her. "Do you have plans tomorrow night?"

Her heart skipped a beat as hopeful anticipation skirted through her. "No. Not unless you count another John Wayne movie Dad will insist we watch. Why?"

"Have dinner with me. Seven-thirty?" He brushed a thumb over her cheek, his eyes never leaving hers.

"Okay," she breathed. "Where should I meet you?"

He shook his head and gave her a tender smile. "It's a date, Abs. I know it's the twenty-first century and all, but if you don't mind, I think I'd still like to pick you up."

"I can work with that." Joy burst through her at his mention of a date, and she had to fight to keep the silly grin off her face.

"Good." He leaned down and kissed her lightly on the cheek he'd been caressing then turned and walked back into the brew pub.

"Holy witch warts," a woman said from behind her.

Abby spun and grinned when she spotted Wanda in her party cart. When had she arrived? She and Clay had been so into each other she hadn't even noticed.

"Is it warm out here, or what?" she declared, fanning herself.

"It's sixty degrees, Wanda," Abby said, taking a seat next to her friend. "Warm isn't exactly the word I'd use."

"Not anymore it isn't. After that public display, I'd say Keating Hollow's core temperature just rose a good twenty degrees."

Abby laughed and shook her head. "Stop. We weren't even doing anything."

"Sure, Abby. If you say so." Wanda put the cart in reverse and started backing up.

"Where are we going?" Abby asked.

Wanda scrolled through her smart phone, and after a second, Taylor Swift started to sing about buying a dress just so someone could take it off. Wanda leaned over, grinned, and said, "To find you something to wear on your hot date."

CHAPTER 19

*A*bby hummed to herself as she slipped into her family home, shopping bags in hand. She and Wanda had spent the last couple hours in Bewitched, the women's boutique on Main Street. After trying on practically every dress in the place, Abby finally went with a red halter top number that did great things for her shoulders and waistline. But it was the shoes that she'd fallen in love with—four-inch heels with silk ribbons that wrapped around her ankles and tied off with a bow. She felt feminine and sexy just thinking about wearing her new ensemble.

The house was dark and quiet. Abby quickly dumped her purchases in her room, checked on her dad, who was napping, and got to work on making him something to eat when he woke up. An hour later, she had soup simmering on the stove and cornbread cooling on the counter.

Abby sat down and turned her computer on. Just as she clicked into her email, she heard her dad's bedroom door open. She turned and smiled at him. "Dinner's ready when you are."

He pressed his palm to his gut and shook his head. "Nothing for me, honey. Just need some water and crackers."

Abby peered at him as he moved into the light. His face was ashen, and dark circles rimmed his eyes. "Did you have another treatment today, Dad?"

"This morning." He shuffled past her, opened the cabinet, and retrieved the saltines.

"Dad, I told you I'd take you. Why didn't—"

"I forgot it was today, and by the time I realized I had the appointment, you were already gone. Yvette went with me."

"Oh. Well that's good. How'd it go?"

"Fine until about ten minutes ago." He reached into the fridge and retrieved a bottle of water.

Abby forced herself to stay seated and not jump up to help him. If there was one thing she'd learned since she'd come home, it was that her dad hated it when his daughters treated him like he was an invalid. "Nauseous?"

"That's an understatement." He paused, and sweat popped out on his forehead as his face turned a sickly shade of green.

"Are none of the potions from Charming Herbals helping?"

"No." He paused, set the crackers and water down, and clutched the counter while he breathed through the obvious wave of nausea.

Dammit! Abby cursed herself. Why couldn't she get her own potions to work? The ones she'd made as a teen had never failed to help settle anyone's upset stomach. She hated watching her dad suffer when she knew deep down she should be able to help.

Her dad suddenly bolted for his bedroom, leaving his crackers and water behind.

Tears stung Abby's eyes, but she blinked them back. Determined to help, she grabbed the crackers and water off the counter and slipped into his bedroom. She set the items from the kitchen on his bedside table, and grimaced when she heard the retching coming from the master bathroom. There was only one thing to do—try again. Only this time, she'd do it in her own space.

It was time to confront her last demon.

Squaring her shoulders, Abby strode out of her dad's room and headed for the kitchen. After she gathered supplies, she made her way outside to the pretty shed her dad had built for her twenty years ago. There was no hesitation; only determination as she pulled the door open.

She'd expected her space to be dusty, filled with cobwebs and traces of other critters who'd taken up residence in her absence, but the space was immaculate. The stainless steel gleamed under the recessed lighting, and her copper pots and bowls hanging from the rack were dust free. There were even rows of fresh herbs lining her shelf.

"Noel did this," she said. "There's no question." Abby shook her head, both mildly annoyed and grateful. Of course she had. Her sister had been pushing for her to get back into healing for years. It made sense she'd make sure her space was ready to go when Abby finally got up the nerve to try again.

Nerves took over, and Abby's hand shook as she pulled one of the copper pots down off the rack. She did her best to keep her eyes trained on her work station, but she couldn't help glancing back at the bench pushed up against the wall. Images of Charlotte flashed in her mind. Her body tensed, and her heart stopped for a moment. It was the last place she'd seen her friend. Charlotte had been sitting right there when Abby had given her the potion—the potion that had ultimately caused her demise.

Abby shook her head violently, forcing the memory from her mind. *Not now.* She couldn't let her dad continue to suffer.

Not when she knew that somewhere deep inside her, she had the power to help him.

Turning her back on the bench, Abby got to work. Thirty minutes later, she held her breath as she said the final incantation. Her magic burst from her with a force so great and bright it sent her stumbling back a few steps.

"Whoa." She grabbed the counter to steady herself and continued to stir. The potion turned vibrant gold. Hope blossomed in her chest as she waited. Five seconds, ten, fifteen, twenty. Just as she was starting to believe she'd finally broken through her mental block, the potion turned beige and gave off a faint odor of rotten eggs.

"Ugh!" she cried, picking up the pot and throwing it across the room. The potion splattered against the wall and dripped down, running onto the bench. Abby stood there, watching her failure stain the shed, a stark reminder of why she'd run ten years ago.

Something inside Abby broke, and a sob ripped from her throat as she sank to her knees and buried her face in her hands. She didn't know how long she sat there on the cool tile floor, unending tears streaming down her face, but when they finally stopped, she felt hollow and weak. She lay down and closed her eyes, cushioning her head with her hands and willing the darkness to take her.

∼

"ABBY? COME ON, ABS, WAKE UP."

"Noel?" Abby's voice cracked as she forced the word out. She blinked, her vision blurry with sleep.

"What are you doing out here? Dad was worried."

Abby rubbed at her dry, itchy eyes and pushed herself up. Pain throbbed in her shoulder and hip. "Ouch."

Noel's red hair fell forward as she reached down and offered her sister a hand.

Abby gratefully took it and hauled herself up off the floor. Once she was on her feet, she glanced around and groaned when she saw the sunlight gleaming through the window. "I didn't mean to spend all night out here."

Noel nodded to the wall behind her. "Looks like you had an exciting evening."

Abby leaned against the counter and grimaced. "More like a frustrating one."

"Want to talk about it?"

Abby shook her head but then said, "Dad was sick after his treatment. I couldn't stand seeing him that way and came out here to try to make the potion again. I guess I thought if I was in here maybe I'd get past whatever's blocking my ability."

Noel turned to stare at the potion dried to the wall.

"I really did try, Noel," Abby said with an air of frustration. "I can't just make it happen. No matter how much you want me to."

"I didn't say anything," Noel said, tilting her head to study her sister. "Not since that day in Bree's shop anyway."

Abby stared at her feet, guilt and shame taking over. "I know. I just… I can't stand seeing dad sick."

"Oh, Abs." Noel reached out and grabbed her hand. "I'm sorry. I should've never tried to guilt you into doing something you're not ready for. This is just hard for all of us." Tears filled her big blue eyes. "This isn't all on your shoulders. I know that, so do Faith and Yvette. I—I'm sorry."

"Oh, man. We're a mess." Abby wrapped her arms around Noel and hugged her fiercely.

"I know." Her sister choked out a half laugh, half sob and hugged her back. The pair of them held each other for a long moment until Noel said, "I think we both might need therapy."

A sad chuckle burst from the back of Abby's throat. "That's what Clay said."

Noel pulled back and gave Abby a confused look. "That we both need therapy?"

"No. He was talking about me. Mrs. P asked me to see someone, too. I think the universe is trying to tell me something."

Noel pressed her lips together and gave Abby a sympathetic smile. "Maybe it's time to listen?"

Abby shrugged. "What do I have to lose?"

"That fifty-pound bag of guilt you carry with you?" Noel said, her eyes gleaming as she teased her. "Your jeans would probably fit better if you unloaded some of it."

"Hey, now! My jeans fit just fine, thank you very much."

"If you say so." Noel grinned, eyeing Abby's waistline.

Abby rolled her eyes and moved to the door. "Stop. And let's go in so I can find some breakfast before I bare my soul to some stranger."

"And coffee. Lots and lots of coffee. It only eight, and it's already been a day."

"You can say that again." Abby held the door open for her sister, and as Noel moved past her, Abby said, "Thanks for what you did here."

Noel cast her a sideways glance. "You mean letting you blubber all over my sweater?"

"No, for cleaning the place up and making sure it was ready for me."

The amused expression on Noel's face vanished and was replaced with sincerity when she said, "I've always believed in you, Abby. And I do now. You loved this place from the day Dad built it for you. And even if you never make another potion in here ever again, that's okay, but you deserve to have your space back. I just wanted it to be here for you when you were ready."

Abby tilted her head to the side as she studied her sister. "Did you just say something nice to me?"

"No. Maybe you need to get your ears cleaned." Then she winked and tugged Abby out of her work shed and into the house.

CHAPTER 20

$\mathcal{C}$lay stood in front of the mirror in his bedroom, attempting to manipulate the blue silk tie he'd decided he needed to wear. He couldn't remember the last time he'd seen fit to dress up in a suit. It had probably been in L.A. for some event Val had coerced him into attending. He wasn't exactly the tie type of guy, and after the third attempt to get the knot straight, he tugged the thing off and threw it into the chair in the corner of his room.

"You look better without it anyway," his mother said from his doorway.

He glanced over at her and smiled his appreciation. She'd offered to watch Olive while he took Abby out. "Hey. When did you get here?"

"Just a few minutes ago. Olive is packing a bag."

Clay frowned. "She doesn't need to stay over. I can pick her up after Abby and I have dinner."

His mother waved an impatient hand. "Forget it. Go out. Have fun. Olive and I are having a sleepover."

Clay nodded, distracted as he glanced at the clock. He was

picking Abby up in thirty minutes, and time seemed to be alternating between standing still and going warp speed. Right then, it was standing still.

"That way you can have a sleepover of your own if you like," his mother said with a laugh.

"What?" Clay jerked his head in his mother's direction. "That's not…" He shook his head. "Abby and I are just getting to know each other again. Sleepovers aren't in the cards."

"Sure, Clay," she said with a chuckle as she floated down the hall toward Olive's room.

Clay grumbled, grabbed his phone and wallet off his dresser, and shoved them into his pockets. Was she trying to ruin his night? The last thing he wanted to be doing was talking about his love life, or lack of one, with his mother.

Abby's beautiful face filled Clay's mind, and all thoughts of his mother vanished. That kiss they'd shared the day before was burned in his brain, and he hadn't been able to stop thinking about her. There was nothing he wanted more than to spend a little alone time with her and see where things headed.

But then as always, the nagging doubts plagued his mind. Would she stay in Keating Hollow this time? Could he afford to let her back into his heart and, more importantly, Olive's? He couldn't let this thing go too far until he knew for sure what her plans were for his and Olive's sake. It was something they'd need to talk about sooner rather than later. He knew that. But he couldn't stop himself from spending time with her. He didn't even want to. There was some sort of magnetic pull between them that wouldn't let him keep his distance—at least for tonight.

Clay walked down the hall to his daughter's bedroom and stood in the open door, leaning against the frame. "Are you packing your entire bedroom?" he asked with a chuckle.

Olive finished packing what looked to be her entire stuffed animal collection into a duffle bag. She glanced up and grinned at her father. "No. But I can't leave my stuffed animals here. They've already spent too many nights alone while I was with Mom."

He pursed his lips and took on a wounded expression. "What? I don't count? I was here with them."

She eyed him suspiciously. "Did you let them sleep in the bed with you?"

"Well, no."

"Did you come in here and tuck them in?"

"Um, no, but they were already in your bed. I figured—"

"Then, no." Olive shook her head definitively. "You being here doesn't count. They're lonely."

Clay stifled a chuckle and nodded solemnly. "I can see that. You're a good stuffed-animal mama."

She grabbed her favorite stuffed dog off her bed and clutched it with both arms as she snuggled her cheek against its sweet face. "Thanks, Daddy."

He moved into the room and crouched in front of her. "You be good for Grandma tonight, okay? I'll see you first thing in the morning for chocolate chip pancakes."

Olive let out a squeal of delight as his mother snorted her bemusement behind him. So what if he was feeling a tiny bit guilty about shipping his daughter off for the night so that he could go out on a date? It wasn't like he dated all the time… or ever since the divorce.

Olive wrapped her arms around Clay's neck, giving him a hug. Then she kissed him on the cheek. "I love you, Daddy."

Clay's heart melted, and he held tighter to his little girl. "I love you, too, little bug."

Just as he let her go, the doorbell buzzed.

"Expecting someone?" his mother asked hopefully.

"Nope. Only you. I'm picking Abby up at her house."

"Oh." She didn't even try to hide her disappointment.

Clay rolled his eyes and strode through his one-story craftsman to open the wide, wooden front door.

"Hello, Clay." Val stood on his porch, holding an envelope.

He stepped outside and closed the door behind him, trying to protect Olive from whatever she was trying to pull this time. "What are you doing here, Val?"

She handed him the envelope. "I'm here for my daughter."

"The hell you are." His fist closed and the paper crumpled in his hand. "Olive isn't going anywhere. She's just getting resettled and has school."

Val glanced down at the envelope. "The judge thinks differently."

White-hot anger coiled in Clay's chest as he glared at her. "What are you talking about?"

"I got a temporary injunction. Olive is coming to live with me until the custody hearing."

She was bluffing. She had to be. He narrowed his eyes at her then ripped the envelope open. Inside, there was a court order stating that Valerie Garrison had temporary sole custody of Olive Garrison. Clay stared at the paper, disbelief rendering him frozen. Then he lifted his gaze and scowled at her smug expression.

"Olive is coming with me." She reached for the door knob, but Clay moved, blocking her.

"How did this happen?" He waved the paper at her. "I wasn't notified of any emergency hearing."

"My lawyer suggested it since you won't let me see my daughter when I want to. He thought you might be a flight risk since I'm taking you to court. The judge agreed since you moved her here without my consent when we split. This way, we can make sure you don't disappear with Olive again."

Her cat-that-ate-the-canary grin made Clay want to throttle her.

"*You* left *us*," Clay said through clenched teeth.

She waved an unconcerned hand. "I was out of the country for a job, Clay. I didn't snatch Olive and move away without telling you."

"You were gone for six months, and you never called us after the first week." Clay's face was so hot he was certain his head was going to explode.

"You knew where I was." She shrugged. "I had to hire a private detective to find you once I got back to L.A."

He stared at her like she'd grown three heads. What in the world was she talking about? Was she so deluded that she'd convinced herself of this insane narrative? "Valerie," he said, striving for patience he didn't possess, "I called and left a message on your phone. You never called us back. My cell number didn't even change. You could've found us at any time with minimal effort."

"It doesn't change the fact that you moved my daughter without my consent, Clay. Now she's coming to live with me for the time being."

"No!" Olive screamed from inside the house. "No! I won't go. You can't make me."

Clay turned and spotted her standing at the open front window. How long had she been standing there? And how much had she heard?

"Olive, sweetheart," Val said, pushing past Clay and opening the door.

Clay had to force himself not to physically remove Val from his property. Any altercation between them would only make matters worse. Instead, he pulled out his phone and called Lorna.

"Clay?" she answered on the second ring. "What's wrong?"

177

He wasn't surprised she was alarmed by his call. He wouldn't be calling after hours if there wasn't a problem. "Val just showed up with a temporary custody order. She somehow convinced a judge I might take off with Olive."

She sucked in a sharp breath. "You're sure it's a real order?"

Clay's entire body tensed. He hadn't even considered she might've lied. "It looks like it to me, but I'm not a lawyer."

"I'm on my way. Do not let her take Olive until I get there."

"I don't want to let her take her at all," Clay said.

"I know. But don't do anything right this minute. I'm already out the door."

"Okay. Thanks." Clay ended the call and strode back into his house.

Olive was clutching his mother's waist, shaking her head *no* while Val towered over her, ordering her to grab her suitcase.

"Val, can't you give her a minute?" his mother said. "You just sprung this on her. She needs some time to adjust."

"She doesn't need to adjust to anything. I'm her mother. Now go on, Olive. We have a plane to catch. Either get your stuff or we're going without it, and you'll have to wear the same clothes all week."

"Valerie!" Clay stalked over to her. "Do not threaten my daughter."

She rolled her eyes. "I'm not threatening her. There are consequences to actions, Clay."

Clay couldn't recall a time when he'd ever hated anyone before. But right then, he felt the hatred for his ex-wife burn through him. "So you're going to punish an eight-year-old by making her wear dirty clothes? What's wrong with you?"

"She has clothes at my house, Clay! I was just trying to make a point." Valerie turned around and held her hand out to Olive. "Come on, sweet girl. Let's go have some mother-daughter time. Just you and me. What do you say?"

Olive lifted her gaze from the floor and regarded her mother with interest that wasn't there before. "Just us?" she asked tentatively, as if the offer was too good to be true. Sadly, Clay feared his daughter was correct in her assumption.

"Sure, baby. We'll go get our hair and nails done, then when we're all dolled-up, we'll be the two prettiest ladies at the auditions I have lined up for us."

The hope in Olive's gaze vanished, and she buried her head back in Marina's stomach. "I'd rather stay here," she mumbled.

"Well, you can't, Olive. It's time to grow up. You're not a baby anymore, so grab your bag and let's go."

"Not yet," Clay said, stepping between them. "My lawyer is on her way. You're not taking Olive anywhere until she inspects the order."

"I have the right to do whatever I want, Clay," she said.

"You can wait fifteen minutes." He crossed his arms over his chest and glowered at her.

"Fine." She stomped over to his overstuffed arm chair and perched on the edge of the seat as she glanced over at him. "Make your daughter go get her suitcase."

"I'm not making her do anything." Clay felt Olive's gaze on him, but he didn't glance at her. If he did, he thought he just might break. The thought of Valerie taking her back to L.A. made his stomach turn. He knew she hated it there, and he hated it when she was away. His only hope was if the court order was a fake. Too bad he didn't believe for a second Valerie would show up with forged documents. She was sneaky, not stupid.

"I'm not going," Olive said, her voice strong and sure as she clutched her grandmother. "I'm going to Grandma's tonight."

Valerie raised one eyebrow and scanned Clay from head to toe, apparently taking in his appearance for the first time since she'd arrived on his doorstep that evening. "And where were you going looking so handsome? Hot date?"

Cringing, he glanced at the clock. He was due to pick Abby up in less than ten minutes. There was no way he was going to make it that evening, but he'd be damned if he'd let Valerie have the satisfaction of knowing anything about his personal life. He'd have to wait until this was settled to call and cancel the date.

Clay moved to stand next to Val. He placed a hand on the arm of the chair and in a low tone asked, "Why are you doing this?"

"She's my daughter, too, Clay. Did you ever stop to think I just want to spend time with her?"

A snarky reply was on the tip of his tongue, but he held it back. Fighting with her in front of Olive wasn't something he wanted to do. Olive was already resistant enough. She didn't need to see them at each other's throats, too. "We'll just see what Lorna says."

"Who's Lorna?" She dragged out Lorna's name, turning it into some strange innuendo. Hadn't she listened to him at all? He supposed not. She never had before, so why would she start now.

Clay gave her a flat stare. "My lawyer." Then he walked over to Olive and held an arm out. "Come here, bug."

Olive released his mother and buried her face into his stomach as she held on with everything she had. His heart shattered right there in his living room. And he knew there was no way he was letting her walk out of his house that night without him.

CHAPTER 21

$\mathcal{A}$bby glanced at the clock and then her phone for what had to be the tenth time. No messages. Clay was over an hour late. As the minutes ticked by, she alternated between being annoyed at being stood up and worrying about what might have happened. There couldn't have been an emergency at the brewery. Someone would've called the house. That meant either Clay was blowing her off or something had happened to keep him from calling her.

He wasn't the type to blow her off. She was certain he'd at least call. The worry she'd been holding at bay got the best of her, and she grabbed her phone and sent him a test.

Hey. Just checking to see if everything's okay.

No response.

Abby put her phone down and went out into the living room to check on her dad.

"Look at you," he said, smiling. "Clay isn't gonna know what hit him." Lin Townsend was sitting in a recliner, his feet up, holding a steaming mug of what she guessed was hot cocoa, judging by the large dollop of whipped cream floating

181

on top. *Good*, she thought. He could use the calories after the last few days.

Abby shrugged. "If he shows up. He was supposed to be here an hour ago."

Her father frowned. "It's not like Clay to be late. Has he called?"

Abby shook her head and flopped down onto the couch. "Looks like you'll have to be his stand-in."

Lin raised his mug. "A night of John Wayne and hot cocoa never hurt anyone."

Despite her growing disappointment, Abby couldn't help but laugh. She'd been spot-on when she'd said her evening would be spent watching another John Wayne movie. "Sounds good to me."

Her dad reached over and squeezed her hand. "I'm sure he has a good reason."

Abby nodded, trying to stifle the worry coiling in her gut. She didn't know what was going on, but she knew it couldn't be good if Clay hadn't even called.

Her phone buzzed, and Abby jumped up to grab it.

Wanda's name flashed on the screen. Disappointment slammed into her, but she forced herself to sound cheerful as she answered the phone. "What's up?"

"Abby, are you okay?" The concern in Wanda's voice was palpable.

"Sure. Why wouldn't I be?"

"Oh, because um... Didn't Clay call to cancel?"

"No. As a matter of fact he didn't." Abby tapped her fingernails on the counter, suddenly angry that Wanda had details she didn't. "Spit it out, Wanda. What do you know?"

"Crap. I thought he must've called you. Dang it, Clay," she muttered.

"Wanda," Abby said with a sigh.

"Sorry, Abs. I was just headed home when I passed Clay's house and saw him and Olive hauling out luggage to a rental car Val was standing next to. Then all three of them got in and drove away."

Abby felt like she'd just been sucker-punched in the gut. "They left together? In the same car?"

"Yeah. I'm so sorry, babe. I um… well, I couldn't resist so I followed them down Main Street, and they were definitely leaving town together."

"You're kidding me?" Abby blurted. "But why?"

"That's a good question. And to be honest, I figured you'd be the one to have the answer. Are you okay?"

"No," she said automatically. Why in the world would Clay be going anywhere with Val? He'd made it sound like there was no love lost between them, hadn't he? "I don't know. I guess I'm fine. It was just a date."

"A date you've been waiting ten years to go on," Wanda said.

"Thanks. I needed that," Abby said, her voice dripping with sarcasm.

"Sorry. Listen, I'm coming over. I'll be there in twenty minutes."

"You don't have to do that. My dad's here. I'm fine."

Wanda let out an impatient huff. "I know I don't have to, but it's what friends do. And I'm not letting you mope around at home because some guy blew you off. Dress in something warm. I'll be there shortly."

The line went dead, and Abby put the phone down. "Dad?"

Her father tore his attention from the television. "Yeah, kiddo?"

"Looks like I'm going out after all. Do you need anything before I go?"

He lifted his mug and his remote. "No thanks. I'm set."

She chuckled and retreated to her room to change out of

the gorgeous red dress. Ten minutes later, she was dressed in jeans, a sweater, and ankle boots. On her way out of her room, she grabbed a knitted hat and a scarf. It wasn't exactly freezing in Northern California in October, but once the sun went down, the temperatures plummeted with it.

"Abby your friends are here," her dad called from his recliner.

She strolled out into the living room, bent to kiss her dad on the cheek, and smiled. "I'm glad you're feeling better today."

"Me too. Now go out and have fun." He waved a hand at the door. "John Wayne has it from here."

"Will do. See you in the morning." Abby grabbed her coat and slipped out the front door.

Strobe lights flashed from Wanda's party cart, and a cheer rose up from the ladies she'd brought with her. "Whooohooo! It's about time we got you out of the house," one of the women called.

Abby squinted. "Shannon, is that you?"

"Sure is." The tall, curvy redhead waved a hand. "Get over here. We have places to go and people to do."

"Shannon, behave." Hanna darted out of the cart and wrapped her arms around Abby. "Hey, you."

Abby grinned and held onto Charlotte's little sister with everything she had. "You're a sight for sore eyes."

"My mom was thrilled you came by," Hanna whispered into her ear. "She hasn't stopped talking about it. She's really missed you."

"I've missed her, too," Abby said, choking back the emotion threatening to overtake her. "She was wonderful."

"Just don't be a stranger, okay? Dad wants a chance to say hi, as well." Hanna let her go and stared her in the eye. "And Candy needs to apologize, the little trouble-maker. I can't believe she had the nerve to just drive off like she did."

Abby followed Hanna over to the cart, and the pair of them slid into the middle row. "If I'd known the mini belonged to your mom, I'd have come sooner."

Hanna raised a questioning eyebrow. "Really? Are you sure about that?"

Abby couldn't blame her for being skeptical. It had taken her ten years to show up. "Yeah. I couldn't let something like that go."

Hanna nodded then leaned forward and said, "Come on, Wanda. We need to get this party started."

Wanda nodded and hit a button on her smart phone. Pink started belting out lyrics as Wanda turned the cart around and headed back down the Townsend driveway.

Abby leaned over and asked Hanna, "Where are we going?"

Hanna passed Abby a bottle of beer and raised her hands in an I-don't-know motion. "Does it matter?"

I guess not," Abby said with a chuckle then took a long swig of chocolate stout brew. A moment later, all three of her friends started singing at the top of their lungs, and Abby felt a weight lift off her chest as her heart swelled with love for her friends. And for the first time in forever, Abby knew she was exactly where she was supposed to be.

The cool air seemed to wash away her worries and disappointment. Her dad was having a good night, and she had her girls. For now, that was enough.

"Who wants to go skinny dipping?" Wanda called over her shoulder.

"Yeah!" her two friends called back instantly.

"You've got to be kidding me. It's like forty degrees out here," Abby said, tightening her jacket around herself.

"Ah, but the river is heated." Wanda turned the party-mobile onto the golf cart trail and barreled over the grass down to the rushing river.

"Since when?" Abby asked, staying firmly perched on her seat as her friends jumped out of the cart.

Wanda cackled. "Since last Samhain when Miss Maple accidentally turned it into a bubbling hot tub. She was trying to impress her new beau and sorta overdid it."

Abby stared at the calm water. "It doesn't look like it's bubbling."

"Oh, it will be." Wanda kicked her shoes off and started to undress. The other two followed her lead.

Abby, still sitting in the cart, stared at them with her mouth open. They were just messing with her. How could Miss Maple have turned the entire river into a hot tub? That would take a massive amount of energy.

"Hurry Abby," Hanna called as she stripped out of the rest of her clothes. "You don't want to miss this. Trust me."

"Oh, hell." Abby muttered and climbed out of the cart. By the time she reached her friends, all three of them were naked and running toward the water. Wanda and Shannon jumped in. Steam immediately rose from the river and the water started to bubble just like a hot tub. "Holy crow."

Hanna, who'd paused, jerked her head toward the water then followed them. She let out a shriek of delight as she slid into the water. She popped up quickly and turned to stare at Abby. "What are you waiting for?"

"I have no idea." Abby laughed. She stripped quickly and ran straight into the water. A shock of freezing cold nearly paralyzed her, and she came up sputtering as she shivered uncontrollably. "What the—you guys are terrible." Abby's teeth chattered, and she flailed, trying to get out of the water. "I can't believe you guys. Cripes that's cold."

"Um, Abby," Hanna said from her spot where she treaded water. "What are you talking about?"

Abby wrapped her arms around herself, her muscles

screaming in protest from the ice cold water still clinging to her body. She glanced at the three of them still bobbing in the water. All three seemed perfectly content. "How can you stand it? It must be just above freezing in there." She reached for her sweater and held it up to her chest, unsure of what to do next. There was no way she was getting her jeans on while she was still dripping wet.

"It's got to be at least a hundred degrees," Shannon said.

"Oh no," Wanda said, turning to Shannon. "She's immune. You have to warm her up."

"Immune?" Shannon repeated. "But how—"

"Her magic must be misfiring," Wanda said. "Do something before her teeth chatter right out of her head."

"Oh... Oh, no." Shannon walked straight out of the water, steam billowing from her flawless skin. She raised her arms and said, "Air of the earth's core, rise and cloak this soul in your warmth."

The earth under Abby's feet heated and within seconds, warm air whipped up and chased away the chill. Abby glanced down at her body, noting it was already dry, and let out a sigh of relief. "Thanks, Shannon."

"Sure. Get your clothes on before you freeze again."

Abby didn't hesitate. She redressed and tugged her coat around her. Shannon dried herself and joined Abby in the golf cart while Wanda and Hanna spent a few more minutes in the river.

"How long has your magic been out of whack?" Shannon asked.

Abby let out a huff of laughter. "Ten years, I suppose."

"Ten—oh." She grimaced. "I'm sorry. It was none of my business."

Abby shrugged. "It's okay. I'm going to have to get used to it if I plan on sticking around here, I guess."

Shannon twisted her still-wet red hair into a bun. "Is that the plan? To move home?"

"I'm not sure. Maybe?" Abby couldn't really imagine going back to New Orleans. Not anytime soon anyway. And now that she'd broken up with Logan, other than her roommate, there wasn't really a reason to go back. She loved the town, but she had to admit she'd missed Keating Hollow, missed her family, missed Clay. The thought of him sent a stab of pain to her heart. How could he have just stood her up and not even called or texted?

"You've been missed, you know."

"Have I?" Abby studied the pretty woman. They hadn't been friends in high school, so she couldn't imagine Shannon missing her much.

"Wanda, Hanna, Miss Maple, and plenty of others certainly missed you. Your sisters and your dad, too. Everyone always talks about you with an air of awe and regret. I don't think you know what you left."

Abby frowned. "Awe? Are you sure it wasn't something more like disappointment?"

"Of course not." Shannon gave her a strange look. "Why would you say that?"

"Do you not know what happened... with Charlotte, I mean?"

"Sure. But that wasn't your fault." Shannon tilted her head to the side as if she was trying to figure something out. Finally, she said, "Listen. I know we weren't friends when we were younger. And I take full responsibility for that. I was... well, let's just say I had some serious self-esteem issues and as far as I could tell, you were everything I wanted to be. It's not fair and I'm not proud of myself, but I took it out on you because I was never going to *be* you. It took me a while to figure out that just being me was enough. Once I finally gave myself a break, life got a heck of a lot easier." Shannon frowned. "And I've been waiting ten years to tell you I'm sorry."

"You were jealous of me?" Abby asked with astonishment. "But why?"

Shannon barked out a laugh. "You're kidding right? Everyone loved you. Charlotte, Clay, Wanda. And you had the perfect family. Not to mention just how talented you were. I swear, it was like you could walk on water and I could barely pass witchcraft 101."

Abby shook her head. "You must have done okay. That air spell you did, the way you saved me from freezing my butt off, it was super impressive."

Shannon gave her a half shrug. "I think I might have a problem with structured learning. Or test taking. Or maybe I just didn't care enough then. Whatever it was, school sucked for me."

Regret and shame washed over Abby. How has she been so clueless? While it was true Shannon hadn't been a friend, if Abby had been paying any attention at all, she might have seen the vulnerable girl beneath the armor. It might have prompted her to try to see past Shannon's defensive shell to the sweet girl she was now. "I'm sorry. But rest assured that nothing was ever as great as it seemed. Our perfect family you saw? It was a mess. After my mom left, things were hard. My dad worked all the time, and it was just me and my sisters trying to figure out why she just up and disappeared."

"Oh, man," Shannon said with a nod. "Yeah, that sucks."

"I'm mostly over it." Abby gave her a slight smile. "As much as someone can be when their parent abandons them, I suppose."

A silence fell between them while they watched Wanda and Hanna splash around in the water. It wasn't long before Shannon retrieved them both a bottle of beer from Wanda's onboard cooler. "Here." Shannon passed her the bottle and reclaimed her seat. "I think it's time to forgive yourself, Abby."

"What?" Abby asked, startled. "For what?"

"For not being able to save Charlotte. I think that's what's blocking your magic."

"I don't... Um, I was never trying to save her. I didn't even know she was that sick."

"I know." Shannon turned to her with wise eyes. "But I bet somewhere deep inside, you think you could have saved her had you known. Maybe if you gave yourself a break, your magic would fall back into place."

Abby didn't say anything as she stared out at the river, seeing nothing but the bright moon shining down. Shannon's words echoed in her mind. *Forgive yourself.* Abby shook her head. "I don't think forgiveness has anything to do with it."

Shannon opened her mouth to say something else, but then she shook her head, appearing to change her mind in mid-thought. "Of course. Don't listen to me. I'm probably just projecting my own crap anyway."

Before Abby could respond, Hanna and Wanda appeared and Shannon jumped up to use her magic to help their friends get dry.

Abby, who was done talking about her magic, turned the music back on, hoping it would save her from Wanda and Hanna's inevitable questions. Her plan worked, and right away they all started singing "Shake It Off" by Taylor Swift. Abby sat back in her seat and relaxed when Wanda climbed back into the driver's seat and asked, "Where to next?"

"Downtown. I need dessert," Hanna said.

"You got it," Wanda said, turning the cart in the direction of Main Street. "There's a flourless chocolate cake with my name on it."

CHAPTER 22

*A*bby sat in an armchair in Doctor Kass's office and eyed the text she'd gotten from Clay for the hundredth time. He'd finally sent her a message near midnight the night before apologizing for standing her up. He'd been vague on the details, but he'd mentioned he had to work something out with Val about Olive's custody. She hadn't been able to stop worrying since.

"Hello, Miss Townsend," Doctor Kass said as she swept into the room and sat in the chair directly across from Abby. The therapist had long, straight, silver hair and a kind face with clear blue eyes. She was dressed in a fitted black suit with silver high heels and looked like a million bucks. Abby hoped that when she was in her seventies, she looked even half as good as the older woman.

"So, what brings you here today?" she asked, resting her hands on her wide mahogany desk.

"My magic is on the fritz."

"Hmm, that concerning." Doctor Kass nodded. "Want to tell me what the problem is?"

Abby chuckled. "I was hoping you'd be the one to answer that."

Doctor Kass gave her a wry smile. "Yes, I imagine you do, but that's not usually how therapy works."

"So I've heard," Abby said dryly. "My last therapist was pretty clear he was only there to listen to me talk—and make judgments."

"Judgments?" Kass's eyebrows shot up. "What kind of judgments?"

"You know, the usual. He spent a considerable amount of time telling me what I did wrong and basically just made me feel worse. I went to three sessions and left."

"Ouch." She leaned forward. "I can't speak to his methods, but I will tell you I'm only here to help you find the tools to deal with whatever you're going through. There isn't a right or wrong, only what is. Sound okay?"

Abby twined her fingers together and nodded. "Yeah. Sure."

"How about we start at the beginning? When did you first notice your magic was off?"

"Last week. I was trying to make potion for my dad, and I couldn't get it right."

"Okay, anything significant happen between the last time you successfully made the potion and when you tried last week?"

Abby let out a humorless laugh. "You could say that. It's been ten years."

The therapist's eyes widened with interest. "Ten years. Wow. Want to talk about that?"

It was on the tip of Abby's tongue to say no, but the entire reason she was here was to sort her magic out. There was no way to do that if she didn't talk about Charlotte. Taking a deep breath, she launched into the story she'd never fully relayed to anyone, not even her other therapist. "I was eighteen, full of confidence, determined be the town healer after getting my healer certification. Humboldt State had already accepted me."

"So you're an earth witch, then?" she asked.

Abby nodded. "Yes. My mom was a healer, and apparently her DNA runs strong in my veins. Anyway, I had already mastered all kinds of potions. Ones to relieve nausea, minor pain, headaches, boost energy. And then the end of the school year came. It was prom night, and my best friend came down with some sort of flu-like illness. She told me it was just an infection and the doctor had her on meds that would clear it right up. Charlotte, that was her name, she asked me to make her an energy potion so she didn't have to miss the prom. Her mom asked me not to give her anything, said the doctors were handling it."

"I take it you obliged Charlotte?" Kass asked.

"Yeah. Charlotte pretended like her infection was no big deal. It was prom and I didn't want her to miss it. She seemed fine except for the shadows under her eyes. It was just one night, you know? So I made her a batch. Actually, the recipe produced enough for two batches. I gave her one and stored the other in my work studio."

"What happened after you gave it to her?"

"We all went to the dance. Charlotte seemed fine. She danced with her boyfriend all night. I remember them laughing as they headed out into the parking lot when it was over. That was the last time I saw her alive." Abby swallowed, trying to force down the lump forming in her throat. "Clay, my boyfriend, and I left and spent the night down by the river. When he dropped me off in the morning just before dawn, I noticed the light on in my studio."

Doctor Kass leaned forward, but didn't say anything as she waited for Abby to continue.

Abby closed her eyes and forced the words out. "When I

opened the door, she was lying on the bench, the second bottle of energy potion spilled all over her dress. Her eyes were open and..." Abby shook her head, trying to clear the image from her mind. It didn't work, and all she saw was her friend's lifeless body.

Warm hands covered Abby's, and the therapist's voice was low and gentle. "It's okay, Abby. It's okay to talk about it. Do you want to continue?"

Abby shook her head, but when she opened her eyes and saw the raw compassion staring back at her, she blurted, "She died in my studio, drinking a potion her mother asked me not to give her. She died because of me. It was my fault. Everyone says it isn't, but I know the truth. She was supposed to be home in bed, resting, healing, and I—I gave her the tools to push herself too hard. The doctors said her heart gave out—likely prematurely because of the energy potion. It was too much for her body to take."

Abby let out a gasp and clasped her hand over her mouth. Hot tears fell down her cheeks and with each beat of her heart, pain radiated through her.

Doctor Kass squeezed Abby's hand, passed her a box of tissues, and gave her a moment to compose herself before she let go.

"Thanks," Abby said, dabbing at her eyes.

"It's tough to say things out loud, especially if we're voicing our fears."

Abby sat back in the chair, her body heavy with fatigue. "It's not my fears. It's the truth. Don't you see that?"

"Can't it be both?" Kass asked without judgment.

Abby opened her mouth to answer but closed it when she didn't know what to say. Was the therapist agreeing with her? That Charlotte's death had been her fault? That pit in her stomach grew, and she pressed her palm to her abdomen, trying to block out the sensation.

"Let's move on from that for just a minute."

"Sure," Abby said, recognizing anything else they talked about couldn't be worse.

"Have you used your magic at all since Charlotte's death? Or is it just the healing potions you have trouble with?"

"I make lotions and soaps. They require a touch of magic, but nothing too intense. Not like the potions I made. They're easy and second nature at this point."

"So your magic isn't broken necessarily." It wasn't a question.

"I don't know. Maybe *I'm* just broken," Abby said quietly.

"Is that what you think?"

Abby wanted to scream. Of course that's what she thought. She'd just said it hadn't she? But she bit back her rage and said, "I think it's possible."

"Which part?"

"What do you mean which part? My magic. It's broken. I stopped using it, so it gave up on me."

Doctor Kass blinked and crossed one leg over the other as she leaned back. "But you didn't stop using it. Besides, magic doesn't work that way. It's not there one day and gone the next. It lives inside you. Whatever was there before is still there. You might just need to learn a new way to access it."

"This isn't helping," Abby said, frustration taking over. "Can't you just give me something for anxiety or something? Maybe then I could relax and figure out what I'm doing wrong."

"Do you feel overly anxious? Panicked at interacting with the world?"

Abby gritted her teeth. "Not usually."

Doctor Kass gave her a patient smile. "Then I doubt anxiety

drugs will do you any good. If anything, they will only numb your magic more. How about we try something different? Something like affirmations."

"Affirmations? You mean you want me to talk to myself?" Abby's shoulders slumped. While Doctor Kass was a thousand times more palatable than her previous therapist, this wasn't what she was expecting. She could've gotten this advice out of any number of self-help books.

"Yes. I'd like you to write out five different things; two experiences you're grateful for, two you forgive yourself for, and one you look forward to. Be specific. Say them out loud each day when you wake up and before you go to sleep. Try it for a week, and we'll see where you are when you come back in."

"That's it?" Abby asked.

"I think that's plenty for one visit." She glanced at the clock, indicating an hour had already gone by.

Abby blinked. How was that possible? She felt like they'd just gotten started.

"We've already made a great start. Rome wasn't built in a day." Doctor Kass smiled and stood up, holding her hand out to Abby. "It was a pleasure to meet you."

"You too," Abby said, a little shell shocked that she'd shared as much as she had and that she hadn't been itching to get up and leave the entire time. Maybe there was something to this therapy thing after all.

CHAPTER 23

𝒞 lay paced his hotel room, his third cup of coffee in one hand, his phone in the other. Lorna had just called to inform him that while the court order for Val's temporary custody was legal, there were questions surrounding the judge who'd signed off on the order. She'd just learned through a colleague that Valerie had been seen out with him on various occasions. There was speculation of an affair.

"Affair?" he bellowed into the phone. "This is how the legal system works? Can't we do anything about it?"

"There's not much we can do unless we can find someone to testify that they know each other and are having a relationship. Most lawyers don't want to get on the bad side of a judge for fear it will hobble them in future cases."

"Son of a..." He squeezed the phone so hard his fingers started to go numb.

"I know it's beyond frustrating, Clay, but if we can find any evidence of the connection, it will help with the ongoing custody battle. So keep an eye out for anything, all right?"

"Fine. How long until we can get back into court?"

"I'm filing an appeal today. I'll let you know as soon as I hear anything. Hopefully we can get in to see a judge by tomorrow."

"Work your magic," he said.

She let out a humorless chuckle. "You can bet your butt I will. Hang tough. We'll get this fixed."

After he ended the call, Clay sat at the end of the bed and glanced at his messages yet again. Nothing other than the one from Abby absolving him from standing her up the night before. When Lorna had arrived at his house, she'd taken a look at the court order and advised him to release Olive into Val's custody. She'd convinced him it was the best move going forward in the custody battle. But Olive had been so upset, he hadn't been able to just hand her off. He'd decided to come along to L.A. to make sure he was nearby should she need him. Valerie, who'd been overwhelmed by Olive's temper tantrum, had reluctantly agreed after Clay had been the only one who could calm her down.

Of course Val hadn't agreed to let Clay stay at her apartment, not that he'd wanted to other than to be near his daughter. So now he was in a hotel five blocks away, waiting for Valerie to text him regarding their plans for the day. He'd overheard her talking to her agent about an audition and had insisted he be allowed to tag along. Val had given a vague answer, but when Clay pressed her, she'd finally agreed. But so far he'd heard nothing from her since he'd gotten into his cab at the airport last night.

Unable to wait it out, he called Valerie.

"Where is she?" his ex yelled into the phone.

"Where's who? Olive?" he asked.

"Yes, Olive. Who else would I be talking about? I was just getting ready to call you. Did you pick her up? Are you outside? You need to get her back in here right away. Our audition is in less than five minutes."

"Wait a minute, Val. Are you saying Olive isn't with you?" His heart started to race, and sweat broke out on the back of his neck. This couldn't be happening. His little girl was not somewhere in Hollywood all by herself.

"No. She isn't. She's with you," Valerie said impatiently. "Stop playing dumb, Clay. It isn't going to go over well in court."

"Valerie, listen to me. I have not seen Olive since last night at the airport. I've been waiting all morning for you to call me. Are you saying you're at some audition and Olive went missing?" Clay grabbed his wallet and room key off the dresser and strode out the door.

"Yes, we're at an audition—wait, Olive isn't with you?" A hint of panic radiated in her voice.

"No, she isn't. Where are you? I'm getting a cab right now."

"But she said… oh my god, Clay. Where is she?"

"I don't know," he said through clenched teeth. "She was in your care." He got into the elevator and nodded to the older woman who was staring at him, wide-eyed. "Where are you exactly?"

She gave him an address in Studio City. Two minutes later, he was in a cab and headed her way.

Clay spent the entire cab ride trying to reach Olive on the phone he'd given her just six months ago so he could reach her when she was with her mother, but each time he called, it went straight to voicemail.

"Damn," he muttered. The phone was dead. Either Valerie had turned the phone off or the battery was dead.

The moment the cab came to a stop, Clay tossed a wad of bills at the driver, jumped out, and started running toward the building. Before he could get to the front door, Valerie strode out, her hair curled and piled on top of her head. She had heavy make up on and wore a formfitting dress that was so low cut he was sure she had to be using double-sided tape just to keep from having a wardrobe malfunction.

"Clay!" she cried and flung herself into his arms.

He patted her back awkwardly, and after a moment he grabbed her waist and forced her to step back. "When's the last time you saw her?"

"About an hour and twenty minutes ago. We'd just—"

"An hour and twenty minutes? What the hell were you doing when you were supposed to be watching our daughter?" He felt the heat crawling up his neck and he had to stop himself from throttling her.

"I had a meeting with my agent. Don't you go blaming this on me, Clay Garrison. If you'd just gotten on board with the acting thing in the first place, Olive never would've run off."

Shock rendered him speechless. He shook his head, truly dumbfounded. He did not have the time or the will to have this fight with her. The only thing that mattered was finding his daughter. "Where is the last place you saw her?"

"In the waiting room. I told her to sit quietly while Manny and I had our meeting. She was in the corner near the television when Manny and I went into his office."

"You left an eight-year-old alone in a strange office building in the middle of L.A.?"

"Don't be so dramatic, Clay. It's Studio City, not the ghetto."

"She's eight years old!" he yelled and brushed past her into the building. Valerie rushed to catch up with him, but she was wearing five inch stilettos and unable to keep up with his long strides.

"Olive?" he called as he tore down the plush hallway. He followed the signs for the open audition call and finally came to a room packed with women and their daughters. He started asking around about Olive but soon realized he didn't even know what she was wearing. He spun around and went in search of Valerie. She'd taken her heels off and was hobbling back to the waiting area. "Ask everyone in that room if they've seen Olive. You remember what she was wearing, right?"

"Of course I do," she said, clearly offended. "She's wearing a pink dress with little white rosettes at the bottom. And matching pink Mary Jane shoes."

Clay refrained from rolling his eyes but couldn't stifle the groan. "She was okay with that?"

"It was for the audition, Clay. How many times do I have to explain to you why I dress her the way I do?"

"I don't know, Val. I guess every time you try to explain to me why you're forcing her to do something she doesn't like to do."

She sucked in a sharp breath, and he could see that she was gearing up to lecture him once again on the opportunities she'd have as a working actor. But he didn't want to hear it. Not now. Not ever again. He held up a hand. "I'm going to check the grounds and see if she's outside. You go back in that room and talk to everyone until you find someone who saw her leave. Got it?"

"Fine. I'll text you if find out anything." She wrapped her arms around herself as she chewed on her bottom lip nervously.

"You do that." He started to walk away, but Val called out, stopping him. "What?" he asked.

"Find my baby, Clay. Please," she pleaded, her eyes filling with tears.

"There's no question about that," he said tersely and silently cursed her. This was her fault, and once he found Olive, he was going to make sure the entire legal community knew about it. As he made his way back outside, he called the Studio City police station. When the woman on the other end answered, he said, "I need to report a missing child."

He gave her all the information he had and was told an officer was being dispatched. Clay ended the call and tried Olive one more time. Still no answer. His insides churned as he circled the office building then the city block. He texted Val to see if she had news. She didn't. A couple of people remembered seeing Olive but didn't know when she'd left.

Panic started to overtake Clay as he rushed from business to business. She wasn't at the convenience store, the laundry mat, the nail salon, or the women's boutique. He rounded the corner and spotted a small city park.

He knew instinctively if she was anywhere, that's where he'd find her. His girl was an earth witch, just like her father. If she needed to get away from the auditions or her mother, the one place that would help her feel better was the park. He dodged two oncoming cars as he ran across the street and entered the wrought-iron gates. To the left was a small bonsai garden and to the right there were roses. He chose to head toward the bonsais. She'd been fascinated by the small trees ever since her grandmother had gotten her one for Christmas the year before.

The further Clay got into the park, the more certain he was that she was there. It was as if he could feel her presence.

"Olive!" he called out. No reply. He moved deeper into the park and tried again. Still nothing. He stuck to the path, and when he came to a foot bridge that crossed a small stream, he paused. "Olive?" he called again, only this time he barely raised his voice.

A whimper sounded from somewhere beneath the bridge.

"Olive!" He jumped down onto the muddy bank and sure enough, there was his daughter, dressed in a pale pink dress, huddled underneath the bridge, tears and mud staining her cheeks. He reached down and snatched her up, hugging her tightly to him. She had mud all over her dress and on her arms and legs, but he didn't care. He'd found her, safe and sound. Nothing else mattered.

"Daddy," she sobbed into his shoulder.

He pressed a hand to the back of her head and stroked her wild curls. "I'm here, sweetheart. Everything's going to be okay."

"Don't make me go back. Please, Daddy. I don't want to do the commercial."

"You don't have to, Olive. I promise. No more acting," he soothed, praying there was something he could do to stop Valerie and her insane insistence that her daughter be an actress.

"I want to go home."

"I know, love. I know." Still carrying her, he climbed back up onto the path and made his way to a metal bench. Once he was seated with her on his lap, he took out his phone and sent Val a short text to let her know Olive was safe and in his care. She sent a message right back demanding to know where they were. He ignored her. A second later, she typed out something about still being able to audition. Every muscle in Clay's body ached to throw the phone into the stream, but instead, he shoved it into his pocket and turned his attention to Olive. "What happened?" he asked gently. "Why did you run off?"

Her bottom lip quivered as she shook her head. "I didn't want to audition."

He brushed one of her curls out of her eyes and nodded. "I know. But did anything specific happen?"

She shrugged. "I told Mommy I wanted to go home, and she yelled at me, told me I had to do this for her."

"I'm sorry, Olive. I know this isn't your choice." He wanted to rage and throw Val under the bus, but he did everything he could to keep his temper in check. He didn't want to be the cause of their failed relationship. Val was still Olive's mother and always would be. "But you can't just run off like that. It's not safe. I was really worried."

"I tried to call, but my phone wouldn't work." She pulled it out of a hidden pocket in her pink dress and handed it to him.

Sure enough, the battery was dead. His phone started buzzing and one glance at Val's name made him grimace. "Come on. Your mama is worried too."

Olive buried her head in Clay's shoulder again, but her body had stopped shaking. He hoped that meant the tears had stopped, too.

Clay carried her back to the office building and wasn't surprised to see the blue flashing lights out front when they rounded the corner. He had to give them credit for wasting no time following up. He'd just about reached the first cop car when Valerie spotted them and let out a cry of relief.

"Olive! Ohmigod, baby, are you okay?" She tried to pull Olive out of Clay's arms, but Olive only clung tighter to Clay and shook her head violently.

"I'm not going with you. I hate you. And I hate that man!"

"Man?" Clay's eyebrows rose in question as all his defenses for his daughter went on high alert.

"That man." Olive pointed to a tall, very tanned man with salt and pepper hair. He was wearing an expensive suit and talking to one of the officers.

"What don't you like about him?" Clay asked.

"He's Mommy's new boyfriend, and he doesn't like kids."

"Boyfriend?" A woman with a high-pitched voice cried from behind them. "You must be mistaken. That's my husband, the Honorable Peter Mathis."

Clay recognized that name from the court order Val had brought him the night before and called Lorna immediately.

CHAPTER 24

*a*bby lay in bed staring up at her ceiling. It had been exactly nine days since she'd last seen Clay. She was surprised by how much she missed him. They hadn't even gone out on a real date, but that hadn't stopped her from falling for him all over again. Ever since she'd driven back into town, he'd been the friend she'd needed. He'd made her heart flutter, her pulse quicken, and when she wasn't swooning over him, he'd calmed her, made her feel comfortable in her own skin again. Comfortable in Keating Hollow.

She'd heard from him a few times. He was in L.A. working out the custody situation with Valerie and didn't plan on returning until he could bring his daughter with him. Abby was proud of him and wished she could be there to support him even though she knew it wasn't her place. The small amount she'd seen of Valerie had been enough to last her a lifetime.

Her bare feet hit the wood floors, and she walked over to the mirror hanging above her dresser. Just as she had for the past week she recited, "I am grateful that Charlotte befriended me the first day of kindergarten, and that all the years we knew each other, we never let anything come between us. I am grateful that Clay has let me back into his life, and that even after all these years, he is still the same person I fell in love with. I regret leaving Keating Hollow ten years ago, and I regret giving Charlotte a potion her mother asked me not to give her. The one thing I wish for my future is to marry a man who loves me for me and to start a family."

What she didn't say was that she wanted Clay to be that man. It just seemed too presumptuous. Or maybe she was too scared to say it out loud. But as each day went by, she could feel her courage building. One of these days, she was certain she'd say it. Just as long as he came back to Keating Hollow. Even her magic was cooperating better. She still wasn't able to make her dad's potion, but two nights ago she had managed to join the girls at the river. This time the hot tub effect was in full force.

"Abby? Want breakfast? I'm making waffles," her dad called from the other room.

"Yes!" She quickly dressed in jeans and a warm, long-sleeved shirt and stumbled out of her room in search of coffee.

Her dad had a pitcher of batter in his hand and was humming the theme song to the John Wayne movie he'd watched the night before. Abby rolled her eyes. "Tonight we're watching *When Harry Met Sally*. I can't take one more western."

"No we're not." He shook his head and poured the batter into the waffle maker.

"Just try and stop me." Abby poured a cup of coffee, added a scoop of cocoa, and topped it off with whipped cream.

"Won't be hard if you keep clogging your arteries with that stuff."

Abby grinned and took a sip of her mocha. "We'll see."

"Sorry, child, but you have plans." He pushed a piece of paper toward her. It said *Cozy Cave, seven p.m.*

"Who am I meeting at the Cozy Cave?" she asked, one eyebrow raised.

"It's a surprise." He placed a waffle in front of her and passed the real maple syrup.

"Dad." She drew out the word. "Just tell me. Is it Yvette? Or Faith? Noel? All three of them?"

He shook his head. "Nope. Now eat. You look a little thin today."

"Nice try." She made a face to let him know she wasn't buying his act for even a second. "Is it you? Because that's a date I wouldn't mind keeping."

His lips twitched. "That's flattering, but no. Clair and I have plans."

Abby glanced at the calendar. "But it's only Wednesday. What happened to Friday night dinner and Sunday morning brunch?"

He shrugged. "She's decided she wants more time with me. And since I have a bunch of time on my hands, who am I to argue?"

Abby sobered. She knew Clair actually meant she wanted more time while they still had it. And good for her for making sure they spent as much time together as possible, but that didn't mean the reminder that her dad's time was likely limited didn't feel like a stab straight to the heart. She cleared her throat. "What are you two love birds doing?"

"Not going to the Cozy Cave." He winked. "Don't want to cramp your style."

Abby stared at him, her mind running away with her. "Logan isn't back in town is he? Because if he is I don't—"

"It's not Logan," he said with a frown. "You think I'd help a pompous ass like that get a date with my daughter?" He visibly shuddered. "No, Abby. In fact, if he sets foot back in Keating Hollow again, I'll have Andrew Baker run him out of town. That's how much I don't like that entitled little turd."

Abby barked out a laugh. "Okay. Not Logan. Well, that's a relief." There was only one person left. Clay. But she didn't push her father any further. She'd rather spend the day dreaming he was already back in town and surprising her with dates. If she was wrong, she was certain she'd still be delighted by whoever was sitting across from her at the table. But if she was right, well... she couldn't think of a better way to spend her day than anticipating see him again.

ABBY HAD BEEN WRONG. SHE HADN'T BEEN ABLE TO FOCUS ON anything other than her dinner date. To make matters worse, she'd spent most of that time obsessing about what she should wear. If it was Hanna or Wanda, she'd look pretty ridiculous showing up in a cocktail dress. But if it was Clay, she wanted to dress up and show off a few of her curves. In the end, she'd opted for a long, black lace top, leggings, and knee-high boots. The ensemble was dressy, but not too dressy, and it was fitted enough in the waist area that she didn't look like she was wearing a lace potato sack.

She touched up her lipstick once last time, grabbed her handbag, and waved to her dad and Clair, who were cuddled up on the couch watching *When Harry Met Sally.*

"Have fun tonight," Clair said, grinning at her. "And thanks for loaning us the movie. I couldn't take one more John Wayne flick. I was starting to consider wearing a gun holster just to get his attention."

"That still might work," Abby said. "Add in a pair of cowboy boots and a hat and you've got the makings of one heck of an evening."

Lin turned to eye Clair and pumped his eyebrows suggestively. "You'd look real cute in a hat, boots, and gun holster. Let's try that out later."

Abby groaned and covered her ears. "I can't hear you. La, la, la, la." Laughter erupted from the couch, and Abby couldn't help but join in. "Just try to keep it PG rated around us kids, okay?"

"You started it," Lin said just as Meg Ryan started to demonstrate how to fake an orgasm on the television.

"Okay, that's just about enough for me." Abby raced to get out the front door.

But before she could get the door closed, she heard her dad say, "I'm the one who's being inappropriate? She's the one who suggested we watch this together."

Abby cringed. She had suggested that. Oops. Thank goodness plans had changed. She climbed into her SUV, grateful it was finally fixed after her fender bender on the first day she'd rolled into town.

Not even ten minutes later, Abby pulled into a parking spot a few doors down from the Cozy Cave. Her nerves were on full display when she stumbled out of the SUV and nearly landed face-first on the pavement, but she managed to catch herself before she went down.

"Well played," Shannon said from a few feet away on the sidewalk.

Abby jerked her head up and felt her heart sink. No Clay. "Hey, Shannon." She forced a smile. "You look nice. You didn't have to get all dressed up for me."

Shannon furrowed her brow. "I didn't."

"Oh, okay. I just meant that dress is incredible. And that slit.

I don't think I'd be brave enough to wear a dress with one that came all the way up to my hip."

"I'm pulling out all the stops tonight." Shannon gave Abby a conspiratorial smile. "I finally got Andrew Baker to agree to a date with me. I'm hoping Mr. Deputy Sherriff might show me what he has hiding under that gun belt."

"You have a date with Andrew Baker?" Abby asked, confused.

"Yeah, why?" Shannon waved at someone over Abby's shoulder.

"I just—" Abby glanced back to see who she was waving at and spotted Clay. He was dressed in dark jeans, black boots, and a steel blue button-down shirt. A slow smile stretched across his face as his eyes met hers.

"You just what, Abby?" Shannon asked.

"Huh?" She turned back around and focused on her new friend. "Oh. I, um, I thought you were here to meet me. But I think I just figured out who my date is."

Clay arrived and put his hand on the small of Abby's back. "You made it. Good."

A shiver went through her as she stared at his handsome face. "And you made it back to town."

"Last night, late." He nodded at Shannon. "How's it going?"

"Good, but I think the temperature out here just rose about twenty degrees, so I'm going to go inside and wait for my date. You two remember to find a private room before you tear each other's clothes off, okay?"

"Shannon!" Abby said.

Clay just laughed. "I'll keep it under advisement."

Abby lightly swatted his chest. "Don't encourage her."

"Why not? She's only speaking common sense."

Shannon's heels clattered on the sidewalk and she laughed as she disappeared into the restaurant.

Abby grinned up at him. "So, why the surprise? Why didn't you just tell me you were back in town?"

He slipped an arm around her waist and started to lead her toward the front door. "I guess I wanted to do something special for you after I had to stand you up."

"You know I'm not upset about that, right? Not at all. You did what you had to do."

"Yeah, I know. But I still wanted to make it up to you." He leaned down, kissed her temple, and then opened the door for her.

At the hostess stand, Clay said, "Good evening. I have a reservation for—"

"Garrison." The hostess smiled up at him then cast Abby a dismissive glance before turning her attention back to Clay. "Your usual table is waiting, sir."

"Thanks," Clay said.

The hostess led them to their table but kept glancing back and smiling at Clay. By the time they were seated, Abby was certain the woman had completely forgotten Abby was even there. She hadn't even handed her a menu.

"Um, okay then." Abby reached for the wine list and smiled when she spotted her favorite label.

"Here." Clay handed her the menu. "I don't know what that was about, but—"

"Oh come on, Clay," Abby said, laughing. "You know exactly what that was about. Little Miss Hostess is dying to get you back to her place. Right this minute, she's planning my demise so she can have you all to herself."

"Really?" He glanced at her then back at Abby as he shook his head. "She's going to have to try a lot harder than that, because you're the only one I want to follow home."

Abby licked her lips, forgetting all about the menu. Who

needed food when the man of her dreams was right in front of her, offering himself up?

But before Abby could say anything Clay grimaced. "Sorry. I shouldn't have said that."

"It's okay." Abby reached out and covered his hand with hers. "I don't mind."

He pulled his hand away and gave her an apologetic look. "The thing is, Abs, I truly do want nothing more than to start up where we left off ten years ago. But things are different now, and I can't just fall back into something without considering Olive."

The crushing weight of disappointment settled over Abby, but she forced a reassuring smile. "Of course not. Olive is your priority. I get that. But does that mean there's no room for you to have a relationship?"

"No, it doesn't." He sat back in his chair as the waitress arrived and took their drink orders. When she was gone, he said, "But it does mean I have to take it easy right now. Last week—everything that went down with her mother—it's a lot, Abs. Olive needs time to adjust, and I don't want to throw anything else at her right now. Especially when I don't even know how long you'll be in town."

"I see." Abby nodded slowly as she recalled the bumpy days in her own young life after her mother had left. It was right about that time that Mrs. P had really stepped in and become a lifeline for Abby. She'd love to be that person for Olive, but she knew Clay's mother would probably fill that role. "I don't want to cause any issues."

"That's not what I meant to say. It's just, there's so much to tell you about what happened in L.A. Can we start there?"

"Sure."

The waitress arrived, and Abby was never so happy to see a

glass of wine in her life. They both ordered crab appetizers and the trout special for dinner.

Once they were alone again, Abby grabbed her glass and said, "Go on. I'm listening."

Clay took a deep breath and dove into the craziness he'd experienced down in L.A. After Olive had been found in the park, everything had come out. It was true that Val had been having an affair with the judge who'd ruled on the temporary custody hearing. When his wife found out, she raised a stink so foul that by the time she was done, the judge had rescinded his custody order and then stepped down. The judge's wife was out for blood and Clay actually almost felt sorry for the man. Almost, but not quite. Not after he'd ruled to take his daughter away from him.

Another judge had given Clay full custody, and Val was only permitted supervised visits. And part of the agreement was that Olive never had to go back to L.A. or participate in any of Valerie's auditions unless it was Olive's idea. Clay also had to give his written consent where the auditions were concerned. It was unlikely Olive would ever be a part of the Hollywood scene again. She didn't like anything about it.

"So, listen. Olive had to get up in court and publicly call out her mother's behavior," Clay said. "I just don't know how that's going to affect her going forward. I don't want to add anything new to the mix until she's on solid footing."

"Don't worry about it, Clay," Abby said. "I'm on your side. You don't need to explain further. Let's just enjoy our dinner, okay?"

He let out a breath and nodded. "Okay. Thanks." Then he picked up his glass and raised it in a toast. "To old friends?"

Abby swallowed her disappointment and repeated, "To old friends."

Their dinner conversation was stilted, and the rest of the

evening was slightly awkward after Clay made it clear they wouldn't be dating. Abby hated that they couldn't seem to find their way back to the easy friendship they'd formed, but she didn't know what to do about it, especially when they were on a date.

Finally, after their dishes were cleared, Abby asked the question she'd been dying to ask ever since Clay told her he had to apply the brakes on their budding relationship. "Just tell me one thing."

"What's that?" Clay asked as he signed the check.

"Why the surprise date? I get why you need to focus on Olive, and I'm totally fine with that, but why go through the trouble of surprising me?"

He frowned, his expression apologetic. "I'm sorry about that. It wasn't until this afternoon that I decided I need to put the brakes on things. Olive had a rough day, and I realized I couldn't do this. Not yet. Maybe if you decide to stick around and if we're both in the same place, we can try again later. But now…" He shrugged. "I don't know what to say. All I know is that I need to focus on Olive."

Abby was silent for a long moment. Then she stood and leaned down to give him a kiss on his cheek. "You're a great dad, Clay. I'm proud of you. Thanks for dinner."

"Abby." He grabbed her hand, stopping her from leaving.

"Yeah?"

He gently kissed the back of her hand and said, "Please consider staying in Keating Hollow."

She wound her fingers into his and smiled down at him. "I didn't say anything while you were talking because I didn't want to make it seem like I was making an argument against your decision to focus on your daughter. But that's not something you need to worry about, Clay. I've already let my roommate know I'm not going back to New Orleans. I'm back. Back home where I belong."

His dark eyes searched hers as if he was trying to decide if he'd heard her correctly. Then he stood abruptly and swept her into his arms. His lips covered hers, and he kissed her so thoroughly that when he let go, her lips were tingling and she'd lost her breath.

A few nearby diners hooted and cheered their approval.

Abby's face heated, but it didn't stop her from leaning in and giving him a kiss of her own. Hers was tender and sweet and full of all the emotion she'd been carrying around with her the last month. He responded, pouring just as much feeling into the kiss as she did. And when they finally broke apart, Abby was trembling. She pressed her hand to his heart. "Maybe one day we'll both be ready for this. Until then, take care of yourself, Clay. And that baby girl of yours, too."

With tears threatening to overtake her, Abby swept out of the restaurant and ran to her SUV, trying to retain her last shred of dignity.

CHAPTER 25

*I*t was a full week before Abby could bring herself to go back to the brewery to gather her soap-making supplies. She'd finally become comfortable working in her shed at her dad's house, and it was time to move everything there and let Clay have his brew shed back.

Her magic was improving every day, but it still wasn't one hundred percent. The fact that she still couldn't make her dad the potion he needed to keep him from getting nauseated irritated her to no end, but she'd finally accepted that she couldn't rush things. Someday her magic would come roaring back... or it wouldn't. What she'd finally learned was that her worth wasn't wrapped up in the potions she could make for people. Yes, she wanted to help, but she could help in other ways, too.

Since her magic was still faulty, she'd taken it upon herself to seek out witches on the east coast that might have a formula that would work for her dad. She'd gotten about a half-dozen packages overnighted, and two had turned out to be promising. They didn't eliminate all his symptoms, but after his last treatment, the nausea had only lasted twelve hours instead of thirty-six. It was progress, and she'd take it.

Abby pulled into the only available parking spot in the brewery lot, the one right next to Clay's Jeep. "Perfect."

She jumped out and braced herself for seeing him again. After the kiss they'd shared at the restaurant, Abby knew exactly what she was missing not being with Clay, and it was really hard to stay away. Even harder, she imagined, to see him and not be able to be with him. It's why she'd stayed far away from the pub. She didn't need to make things difficult for both of them when she was finally comfortable working in her old studio.

But she couldn't stay away from the family business indefinitely, and she needed her supplies if she was going to keep her own business running. The pub was busy, and Abby was both disappointed and relieved when she didn't see Clay behind the bar. *It's probably for the best,* she told herself and hurried out to the brew shed.

The door was slightly ajar, and she heard a young voice inside. She poked her head in. "Hello?"

"Hello," Olive said from her place on a small step stool at the counter. She was wearing jeans and a sweatshirt and had one of Abby's aprons tied around her waist.

Abby's heart melted at how cute she was. "What'cha working on?"

She waved at the box in the corner. "My bunny isn't feeling well. Daddy said I could use the shed to make her an energy potion."

"An energy potion, huh? You already know how to do that?" Abby asked, crouching down to inspect the solid white bunny. The creature lay perfectly still in the box as she petted its head.

"Sure. My daddy taught me." She held up a bundle of herbs. "I just need to grind these herbs and add hot water."

Abby stood and peered over her shoulder. It was a simple energy potion. More like a vitamin boost for the bunny, but since Olive was an earth witch her magic would no doubt give it an extra boost that would have her bunny hopping around in no time. "What's got your bunny feeling so blue?"

Olive grinned. "She just had babies, and she's a little tired."

"How many?"

"Eight."

"Woof," Abby said. "No wonder she's tired. I bet they keep her busy."

Olive nodded. "They eat allll the time."

"Need some help?"

She glanced at the door. "Daddy was supposed to help me with the simmering, but he's taking a long time. Do you think you can do that part?"

"Sure." Abby grabbed one of her copper pots and got to work filling it with water. Before long she had it on the stove, the water bubbling. "Okay, we're ready for the ingredients."

Olive carefully scraped her mixture of herbs out of the mortar while Abby used a wooden spoon to stir.

"Let me know when you're ready to take over," Abby said.

"You're doing fine," Olive said and went back to the sink to clean the mortar and pestle.

Someone's been carefully training this little witch, Abby thought. She was careful and precise. Better trained than she'd been at eight years old, that was for sure. Abby glanced down at the mixture and said, "Olive, I think it's ready for your magic."

Olive pushed her step stool over, climbed up, and peered into the pot. "It needs about a minute longer."

"Really?" Abby gave the mixture another stir and nodded. It still wasn't quite as thick as it needed to be. "Impressive."

Olive beamed and took over stirring her potion. Abby

stayed right behind her, letting her do the work, but keeping a careful eye out. The stove was gas, and anything could happen when one started infusing herbs with magic. Though judging by her obvious magical skill level, Olive didn't need any help from Abby. Still, she was only eight, and Olive had even said her dad was supposed to help her at the stove.

"Now," Olive declared. She squeezed her eyes shut and said, "Magic of my heart, infuse these herbs so bunny gets a jump start."

Abby chuckled at the sweet little incantation, but as soon as magic poured from Olive's hands, her laughter vanished. The magic was erratic, and instead of fusing with the herbs, it started to climb out of the pot and was heading straight for the flames. If her magic joined with the fire, all hell would break loose. On instinct, Abby wrapped her hands around Olive's and used her own magic to help the little girl direct her power into the herbs. Joy suddenly washed over Abby, and she felt something she hadn't felt in years. Pure happiness derived from magic. Olive's happiness as she connected with the earth filled up all of Abby's empty places and for once, she felt completely whole.

Olive's magic instantly reversed course and settled into the herbs, turning the potion grass green.

"It worked!" Olive exclaimed. "Yes! I told Daddy I'd get it right this time."

Abby continued to stir the potion while Olive retrieved a glass jar for storing the rabbit's energy drink. When Olive returned, Abby helped her get as much of it into the jar as possible. Then Abby waved a hand over the small amount left in the pot. The heat vanished from both the pot and the liquid, and Abby grabbed a dropper. "Ready to test it?"

Olive nodded, her enthusiasm contagious.

"Okay." Abby filled the dropper and handed it to Olive. "Go on. See how she handles it."

Olive sat on the floor, picked up her bunny, and gently fed the potion to the new mother. Within moments, the bunny's ears were twitching and she wiggled to get out of Olive's grasp. Olive put her on the floor and clapped in delight as her pet started to explore the space.

"Oh, nice," Abby said as she snatched the bunny up into her hands and handed her back to Olive. "But we can't let her have free reign in here. Too dangerous. Better keep her in her box until you get home."

"Right." Olive carefully tucked her bunny into its box then picked it up and started for the door. "Dad! Did you see? It worked. I did it!"

Clay held his arms out to his daughter and gave her a big hug. "I did see. Very impressive. But still, you should've waited until I got back."

"Abby helped me." She squirmed out of his embrace, handed him the bunny, and ran back to Abby, crushing her with a hug. "Thank you, Abby. Thank you so much."

Abby wrapped her arms around the little girl and gave her a big hug. "Anytime, Olive. Truly, it was an honor to help."

Olive gave Abby one more giant grin and released her. She ran back to her father, took the bunny, and as she flew out the door called back, "See you at home, Dad!"

"How's she going to get there?" Abby asked.

"My mom's waiting for her out front."

Abby chuckled. "You have your hands full with that one."

He stepped into the shed and closed the door behind him. "I think you were the one with your hands full. I saw what you did. You saved her from burning the place down. I'm sorry. She really doesn't have the best control yet. She was supposed to wait so we could do it together."

"It's fine, Clay." She gave him a smile that felt as big as the one Olive had just given her. "Your daughter is... special."

He chuckled. "More like rambunctious."

"That, too. But I'm talking about her magic. You must've felt it. She's powerful. One day she's going to be a force to be reckoned with."

He sobered. "You're right about that. It also means I try to keep her in check as much as possible. Like I said, she should've—"

Abby held her hand up. "No. She asked me if I'd help, and I was happy to. She wasn't going to do anything without someone here to help her at the stove, so if that's what you're worried about, forget it. She was careful even though she's still learning."

"Okay." He blew out a breath. "I just worry."

"As all good fathers do." She turned back to the work station and finished cleaning the pot they'd used.

"Abby?"

She glanced over her shoulder. "Yeah?"

"There's something different about you. I can't put my finger on it, but it's like... I don't know. Like—"

"Like I got my magic back," she finished for him.

"Really? When?"

"Just now." She turned around to face him. "I know this sounds a little crazy, but as I was helping Olive, I realized what's been missing when I cast my spells. And now that I've felt it again, it's living right here." She pointed to her chest. "I'm certain the next time I make a potion it's going to turn out just fine."

He narrowed his eyes. "And what's the thing you were missing?"

"Joy. Pure unadulterated joy for connecting with the earth. That sweet little girl of yours is overflowing with it. She reminded me what it feels like to truly love what you're doing. I won't forget this time."

He glanced back at the door as if he could still see her standing there. When he turned back around, he stepped up to the counter. "Prove it then."

"Are you challenging me, Garrison?"

"Yes." It might have been a challenge, but it wasn't an order. She knew what he was doing. He wanted her to use her magic, solidify what she'd felt so she didn't lose it. It was a technique they'd learned as kids in magic class. He pulled down a clean copper pan and handed it to her. "Make your dad that potion."

"Gladly." Abby was careful to follow her recipe to the letter, and thirty minutes later when she spelled her herbs, magic flowed free and strong from her hands. Her heart was full of love and joy, and everything about it just felt right. The potion turned a brilliant gold and had the scent of calming vanilla.

"I'll be damned," Clay said as she poured it into a jar to take home. "You were right. It worked."

"Thanks to Olive," she said, smiling softly at him.

He took a step closer and wrapped one arm around her waist. "You know what I said last week at dinner?"

"Which part?"

"The part where I said Olive needed time to adjust."

"Yeah." She stared up at him, her pulse racing.

"I think she's adjusted. Now that she knows she's home for good, she's not only getting by, she's thriving. And seeing you two together today... Abby, I have to tell you my heart almost burst right out of my chest."

She lifted her hand and swept her thumb over his lower lip.

He closed his eyes for just a moment. "Stop distracting me. I'm trying to tell you I don't think I can live another moment without you by my side. Without you by Olive's side."

"I know," she said and pressed up on her tiptoes so she could kiss him.

He pulled her tightly against him and held on, burying his face in her neck. "Is that a yes?"

"You didn't ask me anything, did you?" she said with a laugh.

"I'm trying to ask you to be my girlfriend. And when the timing it right, I'm pretty sure I'm going to put a ring on that finger of yours. What do you have to say about that?"

She pulled back to stare him in the eye. "Don't say things you don't mean, Clay Garrison."

"Have you ever known me to do that?" he asked, brushing his thumb over her cheek.

Her heart thundered against her ribcage, and her muscles felt as if they'd turned to jelly. If he let her go, she was certain she'd be a puddle of flesh and bones on the floor. But when she spoke, her voice was strong and steady. "No. But that's a big promise. Not one you can just take back without hurting us both."

"I'm not taking it back. But don't get ahead of yourself, Abs. I haven't asked you yet."

"Yet," she echoed. "That sounds an awful lot like an implied promise. Are you sure you mean it?"

"I'm a thousand percent sure. All this week, all I thought about was you and my dumbass speech at the restaurant. You know what I should've done?"

"What's that?" she asked, relaxing in his arms.

"I should've kept my big mouth shut and trusted my daughter. You know what she said to me that night when I got home?"

"What's that?" Abby asked, intensely curious.

"She asked when our next date was and if she could come."

Abby laughed. "I'd be honored to go on a date with you and Olive."

He shook his head. "Three's a crowd. As much as I love her, she's not invited on my dates with you. Not when all I want to do is this." He dipped his head and brushed his lips over hers. Then he moved to her neck and slid his hand down to her hip, digging his fingers into her flesh. Abby leaned into him, craving his touch, but he pulled back and added, "We can have family day. Picnics in the park. Bike rides by the river. Days at the beach. But our dates? They're all mine."

"That sounds just about perfect, Clay Garrison," Abby said, staring up into his soulful eyes. "When can we start?"

"How about now?"

"Works for me."

Clay grinned, clasped his hand around hers, and tugged her out of the brew shed. As they made their way to his Jeep, he said, "I was hoping you'd say that."

Abby climbed into the passenger seat. Once he was in the driver's seat she asked, "Where are we headed?"

He glanced over at her and gave her a wicked smile. "Sunset Cove."

She should've known. It was the site of their first kiss, their first fight, their first... well, their first everything. It was fitting it would be the site of their first reunion. She gave him a wicked smile of her own and said, "Hurry."

CHAPTER 26

ONE MONTH LATER

a bby stood in her father's kitchen watching Olive and Daisy play cards in the middle of the living room. Olive's new golden retriever puppy, Endora, was curled up on her lap. Clair was sitting on the couch browsing a holiday catalog, and Clay was over by the fireplace chatting up her father. Her three sisters were in the corner, presumably plotting her dad's birthday celebration for the next weekend.

Everyone was happy and full of energy, even her father, who'd had a chemo treatment the day before. Abby had finally perfected her potions, and they were doing wonders for her dad. Ever since the day she'd spent with Olive working on the energy potion for Olive's bunny, Abby had been able to execute just about anything she put her mind to. The difference was now she did it out of love, not guilt. And after talking with Mrs. P, the therapist, Shannon, and even Clay, Olive was to thank for her transformation.

Sure, talking to everyone else had helped her on her road to recovering what she'd lost, but Olive had unknowingly found

DEANNA CHASE

the missing link. She'd be forever grateful to the little girl for helping her rediscover the joy in her magic. Plus, Abby just loved her more than she ever thought possible. They'd formed a bond Abby couldn't even put into words. And every time she looked at Clay's daughter, she thought her heart would explode.

"Hey," Clay said, wrapping his arms around her from behind. "What are you doing over here alone in the kitchen?"

"Making hot cocoa." She leaned back and gave him a kiss on the cheek. "What were you and my dad talking about?"

"Oh, I was just asking him something." He ran his hands lightly over her arms.

"About what?" Abby poured the hot cocoa from the sauce pan into three cups.

"You, me, and New Year's Eve."

Abby frowned as she added the marshmallows to the hot cocoa. "What were you doing? Asking him if I could stay out past curfew?"

He laughed. "Something like that."

She glanced over her shoulder and gave him an odd look. "What are you up to, Garrison?"

He kissed her nose and said, "I don't know what you're talking about."

"Daddy!" Olive called from her place on the floor. "Is it time now?"

Everyone in the room stopped talking and turned to stare at Abby and Clay.

She stiffened and whispered, "Clay, what is happening right now?"

He leaned in and whispered back. "You're about to find out." Then he nodded to his daughter. "Yep. You ready?"

"Yes!" Olive handed her puppy to Daisy, jumped up, and ran over to them. She grabbed Abby's hand and pulled her out of the kitchen and into the living room. Clay followed close behind.

Abby's sisters started to giggle and moved closer, fanning out so that they could all better witness whatever was about to go down.

"You stand here," Olive said, pulling Abby even further into the middle of the room. She stood back and studied Abby. Then she grinned. "Perfect."

Abby watched as Olive then slipped her hand into her dad's and the pair of them positioned themselves right in front of her. They glanced at each other and when Clay nodded, they each took one of her hands.

"Olive, Clay, what—"

As if they'd counted down, the pair of them dropped to one knee at the same time and Olive held out a small, black velvet box.

Abby let out a gasp and had to blink rapidly as her eyes filled with tears.

"Remember when I told you that when the time was right I wanted to put a ring on your finger?" Clay asked.

Abby nodded. "Yes."

"Well, I was pretty certain I was ready to do it that day. But as you know, it's not just me. I come as a package deal."

Abby's gaze landed on Olive and there was no stopping them; the tears spilled down her cheeks. She couldn't help it. Her love for the two people in front of her was too overwhelming. "You know I—I wouldn't have it any other way," she managed to force out in barely a whisper.

"That's good, because Olive has something she wants to ask you," Clay said.

"Olive?" She returned her gaze to his daughter. "What is it sweetie?"

It was then she noticed Olive also had tears in her eyes, but her grin was huge when she asked, "Will you marry my dad so that you can be my real mom?"

Panic filled Abby's chest, and she glanced at Clay, unsure of how she was supposed to answer that question. But he was no help. He was grinning like a fool, just like his daughter.

Abby, needing to feel like she was close to them, fell to her knees and focused on Olive when she said, "I'd love to marry your daddy and be your stepmom. There is nothing in this world I want more than that. Truly. But sweetheart, you already have a real mom. I'd never dream of trying to take her place."

Olive's smile fell. "I can't have two moms?"

"Of course you can. Being your second mom would be my honor. I just..." She looked to Clay for help.

He tightened his fingers around hers and whispered, "You're doing fine, Abs."

She nodded and returned her attention to Olive. "Do you understand, sweetheart? Your mom will always be your mom. And I'll be—"

"My second mom," Olive finished for her. "Just like my friend Ashley. She has two moms and two dads." Olive's brow creased with worry. "But I don't want two dads. This one's enough."

Everyone around them laughed.

Abby chuckled. "You're right about that. He's a handful for sure. But I think he's worth it."

"So is that a yes?" Clay asked as he opened the velvet box. A shiny diamond winked up at her.

"Yes, yes, yes, yes!" Abby said and tugged her hands out of theirs in order to give them both a giant hug. As Clay, Abby, and Olive held each other, a cheer rose up around the room.

"It's time to break out the Champagne!" Yvette called.

"I'll get the glasses," she heard Faith chime in.

SOUL OF THE WITCH

"I'll get the cake." Noel added.

Olive wiggled out of her embrace and ran toward the kitchen. "I'll help! The cake's outside in the second refrigerator."

Noel held her hand out to Olive and said, "Lead the way, little Garrison. Let's find that cake."

Clay let Abby go and plucked the ring from the box. He glanced up at her and grinned as he slid the ring onto her finger. "Are you free New Year's Eve?"

"It would appear so." She eyed him. "How long have you two been planning this?"

His grin vanished, and he turned serious as he said, "I can't speak for Olive, but I've been planning this since I was thirteen."

Her heart melted into a puddle right there on the floor between them. "I was twelve."

"Abby," he said as he bent his head and kissed the ring now lodged on her finger. "We were always heading to this moment. No matter where we were or who we were with, we were always going to end up here. It's right in a way that no other relationship has ever been or ever could be. And I know our paths took a few left turns—"

"U-turns," Abby said with a smile.

His lips twitched with amusement. "That sounds about right. But without those turns we wouldn't have Olive or the wisdom to know just how special this relationship is. I know it took about a decade longer to get here than we thought it would, but I wouldn't change it for the world."

Love burst through her and this time, her embrace was only for him. He wrapped his arms around her and they stayed molded together, still kneeling on the living room floor, until Olive arrived with two pieces of engagement cake in her hands.

"Here," she said, thrusting the plates at them. "Aunt Yvette says you two need to eat to keep your strength up for later tonight. What's happening tonight?"

Clay let out a choked laugh while Abby cast a glare at Yvette, who was chuckling to herself while cutting cake.

"Golf cart races," Abby said. "Wanda and I are finally going to see whose cart is faster."

"Ohhh!" Olive clasped her hands together with pure glee. "Can I come?"

"Sure. You can be my second." Abby winked at Clay, who just shook his head. He didn't understand the appeal of the party cart she'd purchased and tricked out with flashing LED lights and a surround sound system. But that was okay. He didn't have to. Olive loved it and so did she.

"Yes!" Olive pumped a fist and ran back to the kitchen to get her own piece of cake.

Clay put their cake plates on the coffee table and held out a hand to help Abby up off the floor. When he had his arms around her again, he whispered, "Don't wear yourself out. Yvette's right. You're going to need your strength."

A small shiver of anticipation flitted through her. She threaded her fingers through his thick hair, and in a husky voice she said, "Don't make promises you can't keep, Garrison."

His eyes sparkled with mischief as he asked, "Do I ever?"

"No," she breathed and said, "Now kiss me."

He pressed his lips to hers, and finally she was home.

DEANNA'S BOOK LIST

Pyper Rayne Novels:
Spirits, Stilettos, and a Silver Bustier
Spirits, Rock Stars, and a Midnight Chocolate Bar
Spirits, Beignets, and a Bayou Biker Gang
Spirits, Diamonds, and a Drive-thru Daiquiri Stand

Jade Calhoun Novels:
Haunted on Bourbon Street
Witches of Bourbon Street
Demons of Bourbon Street
Angels of Bourbon Street
Shadows of Bourbon Street
Incubus of Bourbon Street
Bewitched on Bourbon Street
Hexed on Bourbon Street

Last Witch Standing Novels:
Soulless at Sunset
Bloodlust By Midnight

Crescent City Fae Novels:
Influential Magic
Irresistible Magic
Intoxicating Magic

Witches of Keating Hollow Novels:
Soul of the Witch
Heart of the Witch

Destiny Novels:
Defining Destiny
Accepting Fate

ABOUT THE AUTHOR

New York Times and USA Today bestselling author, Deanna Chase, is a native Californian, transplanted to the slower paced lifestyle of southeastern Louisiana. When she isn't writing, she is often goofing off with her husband in New Orleans or playing with her two shih tzu dogs. For more information and updates on newest releases visit her website at deannachase.com.